# Nothing Happens by Chance!

umSinsi Press
PO Box 28129
Malvern
4055
Kwa-Zulu Natal
South Africa
www.dancingpencils.co.za

ISBN 978-1-4309-0059-7

# Nothing Happens by Chance!

## Catherine de Waal

# Dedication

*To the memory of my beloved husband*
**Stuart Angus Morrison**
*Who believed in me and my writing.*
*Without you, my books would never have been born.*
*Thank you Sam.*

# Chapter 1

It was a child-lock on her shiny electric hotplate that had got Vivienne to where she was. She was married now to Ivor Murphy, an artist currently at work in his own studio. She stood in the small kitchen with bright-yellow curtains, just looking at her hotplate and thinking … the initial attempt at getting her new hotplate to work had failed, because the child-lock had been on and she didn't know how to unlock it. And that was why she was here in Kalk Bay, because her son, Steven, had told her it would be so much better for her here and she figured he could help her with things like that.

Then there was the second incident with the child-lock that had taken her to visit Ivor to get help. One way or another, that child-lock had had a lot to do with her life today.

She smiled. She had made an early pot of coffee for Ivor, along with a tasty breakfast, but Ivor had long gone to his studio. Another cup of coffee and she would decide what to do that day. Much had happened in her life and today was the first time she was able to sit quietly and think about her day. And all that had happened.

Her son, Steven, lived in Paris with his wife, Mariette. Two days ago they had had their first baby. She had seen the picture. A demure little girl in a soft pink blanket with chubby pink cheeks. Vivienne smiled. Her first grandchild, even though her grandmother was far away in South Africa.

And then she and Ivor had only recently got married. Very quietly, but Ivor wanted the coffee shop owner, Charlie Jenkins, at his wedding, because that was where he first set eyes on Vivienne.

"I knew you were special, but I never expected to marry you," he had said softly, only this morning, smiling at her,

"Me, neither," said Vivienne with force. "I remember being most ungracious to you. I'm surprised you spoke to me again after our first meeting."

"I am not. You fascinated me from the time I saw you in the coffee shop looking at the paintings." Vivienne had shaken her head and in the kitchen she had stood up and given him a hug. "It took some time to break through your reserve," she said. "But the wait was worth it."

"And I liked it that we had our reception in that Convention Centre in Rooi Else with the artists I recently taught and with Julie present. And Lady Lavender, who was qualified to be a minister at births, deaths and marriages. She was pleased to see us commit to one another."

They had looked at one another and they had both said, "without Maureen this time."

Maureen, one of the learner painters, had had her evil eye on Ivor, but with all her machinations it hadn't worked and Ivor and Vivienne were now married and very happy together. Now Vivienne sat in her kitchen with a second cup of coffee, shaking her head at the shiny black glass electric hot plate and thinking where a similar one had taken her. From her previous home in Cowies Hill, Durban to Kalk Bay.

Vivienne had within the last year, moved to Kalk Bay and owned a charming small townhouse in the centre of Kalk Bay. She and Ivor had considered where to live after they had married. Vivienne was nicely settled in her townhouse, and the bedroom was large and spacious with a king-size bed and ample cupboard space, plus an en suite bathroom.

Ivor, on the other hand, lived further into Kalk Bay and his house was full of paintings, framed and partly painted. Vivienne had considered moving in with him, but logic told her that Ivor was best left to paint in the way he was used to painting, and that he should in essence use his previous home as a studio and move in with Vivienne. This had, in the end, been the perfect arrangement. This enabled Ivor to paint in his normal way, and Vivienne to get up before dawn each day and from her lounge window, watch the sun rise across False Bay.

It wasn't normal for her to sit and do nothing, but the tumultuous pace of the last week needed her to sift things out. To get priorities right. A correct entry into the new world as Mrs Ivor Murphy required some thought. With horror, she thought of her three erstwhile friends at Cowies Hill, who were so averse to her move ... she had entirely forgotten to tell them of her impending marriage or even to have invited them to be present. She needed to attend to that.

Mariette and Steven had been wound up in the last stages of her pregnancy and were content with a quick call after the wedding. There were no facilities for Zoom at the Convention Centre.

The best thing, thought Vivienne, was to establish some routine that was easy to keep. Like making the big bed immediately, so that the bedroom looked tidy, and washing the dishes immediately so the kitchen was a place to want to be in. Neither of them would make an undue mess in the house, so vacuuming once a week was enough.

*I do need to see I have always enough of the right food stuff stored in the freezer or cupboards so I can make little special treats which I know Ivor likes*, she thought. *And keep a stock of crystallized melon, which I know he loves.*

It was nice, Vivienne thought, to have someone to spoil to some degree. To make happy. Ivor had looked after himself and one could see that he hadn't made a great job of it. She had noticed when they first met that though his shirt was clean there was a button missing. She didn't mind sewing on buttons and looking after Ivor better than he had done, so that he could get on with his paintings ... and look after her.

This she knew he loved to do.

*We are to go out on painting trips at least twice a week*, he had told her. *There are lots of beautiful places around the Cape ... mountains and gardens and...*

Vivienne sat with her eyes shut. She was smiling. What changes in her life! Here was a kind man, a loving man, who was slowly finding that the world was a safe place and he could take chances with his feelings ... and he had a car and would take her out painting wherever she wanted to go.

Sitting thinking about what she needed to do involved telling Jenny, Muriel and Henriette that she had married ... and forgotten to invite them to the wedding. She dearly wanted to see Julie again, to maybe paint with her somewhere that suited her and Ivor. The beach, where the penguins were known to live, or amidst the mountains. She had enjoyed her brief encounter with Julie. Julie had been at their quiet betrothal that Lady Lavender had officiated and at the reception at the Convention Centre. Vivienne felt that Julie painting with them would add to the day's pleasure ... she would suggest that to Ivor and see what Julie had to say about it.

She was so blessed ...and it was a relief to her that Steven and Mariette had weathered the hazards of her pregnancy and they now had a perfect baby girl.

They were not yet married and she knew that Steven would want her at his wedding. Her and Ivor. That was another major step, they both would need to take.

So much going on. Priorities again. She knew action was better than sitting around, so she got up and attended first to the bedroom then to the kitchen, but she had this nagging thought that asked her to call her three friends from Cowies Hill and tell them she had married ... and why she had not invited them to the wedding, which was dreadful of her.

Funny she hadn't thought of them recently, but good friends stay good friends, so once she had her house tidy and had thought of telling Ivor she'd like to paint with

Julie somewhere, the day was free. A phone ... no three phone calls ... to make.

Who first? Not Henriette. She dreaded that phone call. Jenny would be the easiest. So she put a call through to her.

Jenny was ecstatic to hear her voice. "I've thought of you so often," she said. "How is it in Kalk Bay?"

There was the hint of criticism , until Vivienne said, "Jenny, I got married last weekend. I should have called you, but it was a very small gathering." She didn't add that she had forgotten about her three friends at Cowies Hill. "And it would have been very far for you to come. I'm sorry now to just spring this on you."

"Goodness, Vivienne. You ... married ... I can't imagine it," said Jenny. It wasn't very complimentary thought Vivienne, but she let Jenny ramble on. "You are so reserved, unapproachable almost, Vivienne. I imagine it would have been hard for a man to connect with you."

"Well, that is very honest of you, Jenny," she found herself saying, "and yes, I am not a social person but, you see, I have married a man who is also not a social person, so that makes sense, doesn't it?"

For Vivienne this was a long speech. She normally didn't interrupt Jenny's rambles. But, this time, Jenny had her ramble fixed on Vivienne. "Good heavens, Vivienne, this is a big surprise." She carried on for a while then she said, "So please tell me a bit about this man who has stolen your heart." She said that with a kind of a giggle and Vivienne knew that in reality Jenny would love it if a man stole her heart. However, she talked too much... a man wouldn't be able to get a word in even though she was a nice person.

Vivienne briefly filled in a couple more details. "He's an artist, Jenny. He paints beautiful pictures that art shops and other businesses sell ..."

"An *artist*. How romantic," raved Jenny. "I'm sure there's a whole story to tell ..."

But Vivienne wasn't going to be drawn in any further to talking about Ivor or their lives. "Probably," she said to Jenny. "But not now, Jenny. I just wanted you to know and to apologize for not letting you know sooner." Then she added, perhaps unwisely, "If you are ever down this way, do call in on us. It was nice chatting to you, Jenny. Bye for now." And she was relieved to hear Jenny put down the phone.

Now to call Muriel.

Muriel was equally astounded. "You, Vivienne. *Married*. I cannot imagine it, Vivienne. You are so much your own person. So independent. Why would you involve yourself with a *man*," she asked, with a degree of scepticism in her voice.

Vivienne noticed she didn't congratulate her, as Jenny hadn't, which was a relief, in a way, as it cut the conversation short.

"Stranger things have happened, Muriel," she said, "and I really just wanted to apologize for not letting you know and inviting you to our wedding, but it was very small and put together in a hurry. Just a few people." Then she added, "I married an accomplished artist with lots of admirers, but not many close friends."

"Ah," said Muriel, "that makes more sense, but all the same I would think it unwise at your age to *marry*."

Vivienne wanted to end this conversation, so she said, "Thanks, Muriel, but I know I'll manage." Then she added, "If you are ever down here, please call in."

"Thank you," said Muriel with an audible sniff. "But I never move from home." On this note, they ended their call.

Vivienne by now was feeling rather unnerved. What would Henriette have to say? She cautiously rang Henriette's number.

To her surprise, Henriette was overjoyed to hear her voice. "I've missed you so much, Vivienne," she said.

"Those lovely lunches you gave me and those lovely chats we used to have." Vivienne felt a sense of surprise at Henriette's warmth. Before Henriette could say more, Vivienne said, "I'm phoning to apologize ... I got married last weekend, Henriette, and I so regret not letting you know beforehand."

Henriette gasped. "You? Married? Vivienne, I can't believe it. And you won't believe my news either . I've met a man and I'll be getting married too."

Vivienne held the phone in disbelief. The call she had dreaded most was turning out to be the most enjoyable.

"Henriette, how wonderful. How did you meet him? And what is he like?"

Henriette was brimming over with enthusiasm. "I met him at a therapy group. You won't believe it, but I joined one. After you left, I got to thinking that I must have been terrible company for you, always seeing the worst in every situation so I joined a therapy group, and this lovely man, his name is Theodore, was also in it. He told me to call him Ted, but I like his full name. He had the opposite problem to me. He lived in a fantasy world where everything was rosy. He couldn't believe a person would con him out of money or possessions. But it happened to him. So he had to get to grips with the not so nice side of many people. So we both had adjustments to make…. And we liked each other. A lot," she said, and she laughed.

Vivienne didn't think she had ever heard Henriette laugh.

"And he likes my green eyes… his eyes are a very deep shade of blue. Like the depths of the ocean. And we are getting married."

Vivienne was holding the phone with awe … how wrong can a person be?

She managed to say with great sincerity, "Henriette that is the best news I've had in ages. I always enjoyed you, even though you told me such bad things about Kalk Bay …" and she hesitated "… which is why I apologize. I have not been in touch… simply because I wasn't ready to hear bad things about Kalk Bay, because at one time I thought you could be right!"

Henriette was really contrite. "It was only through therapy that I discovered what a negative influence I had been, so I don't blame you, Vivienne. But it is lovely to hear you and so exciting to know that you are now married." Then she paused and added, "He must be very special. You would not marry anyone who wasn't."

Vivienne felt a warm feeling for Henriette. She had so often wondered why she invited her to lunch on a weekly basis, but, deep down, she must have known that a lovely warm person lay behind those deep-set green eyes.

Involuntarily, she said, "If you are ever down this way, Henriette, you and Ted must visit."

"Thank you," said Henriette. "Theodore is a darling. He is a musician and writes music, and sometimes songs as well. That was why he lived in this fantasy world of his music and his imagination. He had to find there is a real world that is not so rosy. But thank you. I don't think it is likely but it might happen."

After a bit more small talk, she rang off. Vivienne was bemused at the three different responses she had had. But she was glad she had made the effort. Although they were not deeply personal friends, they had added variety to her life. For now, she had the rest of the day to fill in as she wished. What to do with her time? She had to remember it wasn't just her alone now. There was Ivor to consider. But he had told her that twice a week they would go out in the car to enjoy the time together and to find somewhere that they would both like to spend time painting.

She had enjoyed the visit to the Mowbray Mill, but she was drawn back to the week she had shared with Ivor at Rooi Els … and which is where they had met Julie. Julie with her photographic studio and she painted.

Yes. She would phone Julie.

"Vivienne," said Julie's warm voice. "It's just a week since you and Ivor got married. It was so special to have your reception at the Rooi Els Convention Centre ..."

"It was very quiet," said Vivienne, "but I don't know anyone here other than Lady Lavender and Ivor, and he has very few friends, so it was very small."

"It was so nice that he invited the people who were at his art course," Both she and Vivienne said at the same time, "except Maureen."

"Yes, and Ivor has had such good reports from the students that the organization want him to hold another one-day training in about a month's time... he is choosing just two of them to paint with us that day."

"Maybe he might like to include them on a practice run," said Julie.

"It's an idea and I'll chat to him when he comes home. He doesn't spend all day at his painting venue. He is home for lunch." She smiled to herself, thinking, *we love being together and he gets home as quickly as he can.*

"Then sass him out," said Julie, "and let me know."

"Yes, and thanks for the good idea," said Vivienne. She was smiling as she rang off. Julie always made her feel good and it was an idea ... she wasn't sure what Ivor would think of including artists on his day out with her.

It was getting on for lunch time. She usually found some tasty easy dish that Ivor could enjoy as he had discovered that he too liked good food. So she had prepared a full lunch for them both. Her savoury tarts were always most welcome, filled with a variety of tasty ingredients with bits of bacon and some herbs to give it an extra delicious taste.

She loved having Ivor to cook for and was happy when she heard the purr of his large open car as he drove up and parked in the lane outside her kitchen door. She listened to the car door opening and shutting, the ping of the alarm and then his steady and fairly rapid footsteps. *He's keen to get here,* she thought, and was smiling as he knocked on the door.

As he came in and she closed the door, she hugged him. She was pleased that he warmly hugged her back. This was such an exciting journey, being married again in her mid-fifties... something she had never envisioned happening. Ivor also gently kissed her. She was getting used to his slightly tickly beard, which she loved.

With his arm still around her he said, "Can I smell something delicious cooking?"

"Yes, Ivor, and I've waited to share it with you. Let's eat, shall we?"

She had set the table in the dining room and they sat down to a relaxed lunch.

"How did your day go?" she asked Ivor, not expecting anything different.

"Very well," said Ivor, "the Art Committee actually came round to visit me. Lucky, I have those frozen almond cakes, so I could entertain them... they wanted to see my work and premises and were delighted with both. And yes, the exhibition is still on, and soon too."

"Well, that's wonderful," said Vivienne.

In between a mouthful of savoury tart, Ivor said, "And your day? I can tell you have something to tell me."

"Oh yes," said Vivienne. "I got courage and phoned the three friends I used to entertain on a weekly basis back in Cowies Hill. I didn't keep in touch, because they were all so negative about me moving here... but I thought I needed to tell them I was married ..." She said this with a kind of surprised expression and Ivor laughed.

"Embarrassed, are you?" he said, with an amused smile.

"Not really," said Vivienne, "but it does feel strange."

"And what did they say?"

"Strangely, the one I thought would be most difficult amazed me. Henriette has changed, through therapy, and she has met a really nice man and is getting married."

"And she invited you to the wedding?"

"No," said Vivienne, "but I did tell her they are welcome to visit if they are ever here. He's a musician." she hastened to say, as Ivor had stopped eating and was looking at her in surprise.

She hurried on, forgetting to eat in her desire to tell him about Julie. "Then I phoned Julie. You did say we could go out together and paint somewhere we both like and I felt it would be nice if Julie joined us. Do you mind?"

Ivor was interested in his food, with salad and whole-grained bread, but stopped to listen.

"Julie thought you might like to also invite a couple of your painting students to all paint together."

"That might take some organizing," he said, "but it's a good idea… maybe not down at Rooi Els, as they all live locally. Maybe Julie could come here… we could run it in my venue, which is big enough. So for another weekend that sounds good, but I'd like it if just you and I go out together," said Ivor, looking at Vivienne. "Without Julie, although she is very nice … just you and me."

Vivienne felt a great wave of affection. Ivor wanting the outing just for the two of them. She was going to understand she had a man in her life and his wants were to be equally as important as hers.

She put out her hand and touched his arm. "Ivor, I love the idea... Julie can join the group in your venue... it is just about you and me now, isn't it."

He smiled at her. "Yes, Vivienne, I'd like you all to myself..."

Vivienne felt that warm sensation again that Ivor brought to her. How lovely it was to have him to herself every day and every night. She smiled as she thought of how awkward she had felt having a man in her bed again after twenty years. He had probably felt the same, but it hadn't taken long for them to learn to enjoy the comforting feeling of having someone to snuggle up to. To keep her toes warm.

She came back to the moment as Ivor was finishing his lunch.

"Have you anything planned for this afternoon. Vivienne?" he asked, as he folded his napkin and put it neatly on the table.

"No," said Vivienne. "I hadn't got past lunch time. I was wrapped up in that."

"Then let me help take the dishes to the kitchen and help you tidy up… as I know you like things tidy … then let's go out in my car and go for a nice long drive … maybe no painting today, just tea in some cosy little place we find."

"Wonderful," said Vivienne … and they were soon had the dining room and kitchen in order and were off in Ivor's open car.

"Where to, my lady?" asked Ivor.

"I don't know the Cape as well as you, Ivor, so you choose."

"What about driving over the mountains, down to the coast on the west where we painted so well … there are beaches we can walk on, and I know a great café with a beautiful view as the sun sets. Perhaps we have an early dinner there … What do you say to that?"

Vivienne couldn't think of anything better. Gone were her thoughts of Steven … of course she loved him. He was her only son, only child, but he was a grown man with a baby of his own and he was free to live his life as he wished – as was she.

They were standing in the kitchen, which seemed the favourite place for hugs, as Vivienne, lent forward and gave Ivor an enormous hug … for which he bent and kissed her.

"Oh, Ivor, I can't think of anything better," she said. "Let me fetch a windcheater as it could be chilly by the time we come back ..."

Soon they were off with Ivor driving his car first along the coastal road next to the ocean, then he turned it towards the mountains and drove inland and up over the mountains.

The vista for Vivienne was very different with an untamed landscape of mountain plants amidst rocks. Proteas and Ericas and small colourful wild flowers peeped at her as they drove along. There was no sign of habitation. After a while, the road dipped and they were driving down the other side of the peninsula. Now far in the distance and below them, she could see the blue of the sea with its frills of white where waves broke on the shore, along with the white of the beach sand.

The wind whipped Vivienne's face and she tied her scarf more securely round her neck.

Soon the car was winding downhill along narrow tarred road, to eventually reach a small town where Ivor turned off to the right.

"I know these places very well," he said. "And this again has a nice beach almost flat, and we can go for a good long walk first ... then opposite is the cafe with delicious hot meals where we will enjoy our supper with a glass of wine, to celebrate ... *the joy of living."*

Ivor parked his car under the shade of a tree. Vivienne got out while Ivor rolled the sunroof into position and locked the car.

"Come, my dearest wife," he said, with that little smile that disappeared into his beard as he looked down at Vivienne. "So petite and such a rock." He put his arm around her; Ivor was not at all talkative and here he was opening up to her.

He said as they walked towards a small gate that opened onto the beach, "It has all been so busy, Vivienne. So many people and things to do. I felt like I needed space in my life, but this space now includes you." Again, he looked at her and smiled that twinkling smile, making her feel warm inside.

Vivienne didn't reply. She needed space herself. She had a responsibility now not just to herself, but to Ivor. A man who had been solitary, and now was beginning to investigate what a fuller life, a life with a wife, meant. Vivienne decided to let him do it his way, as they began walking towards the beach.

Vivienne felt another warm rush of affection for this man, usually so quiet and centred. They had gone through the gate and had reached the soft white sands of the beach. Ivor took his arm away from Vivienne to help her over some big loose logs lying on the beach. Vivienne looked out at the sea. The blue sea with large rolling waves that broke onto the beach was expansive, with its blue almost the same shade as the sky.

She and Ivor were the only two people on the beach. Ivor gave a huge sigh. He put his arm around Vivienne again and drew her closer to him.

"This is what I needed, Vivienne. The white foam of the blue sea, the blue sky and the endless white sands, and just you and me. For me, this is all so new. I've never had a close relationship with anyone, and I'm not really comfortable with myself, so please forgive me if I seem uncaring. I am not. Just new things in my life."

Ivor stopped walking and looked at Vivienne. She was feeling enormous love for this man and snuggled closer to him.

"Ivor, I just love having you in my life," she said. There was a small chill wind and she zipped up her windcheater. "The wind and the sand and the sea and you .... It is all a bit much for me," she said. "I usually spend time in my kitchen."

She laughed, breaking the slight awkward feeling of Ivor opening up when it wasn't normal for him.

The cleansing he had done as a result of their visit to Lady Lavender was having an effect on Ivor.

Ivor pointed to a distant view of large rocks in the sea. "How do you feel about a brisk walk to those rocks, then back again? It will take a good half-hour to reach them … and by the time we are back, we will be ready to visit the café on the opposite side of the car park."

The rocks, which disappeared from time to time in the large waves that broke over them, looked very far away, but Vivienne agreed. A brisk walk and no talking was what she needed as well. Ivor, with his long legs, walked much faster than Vivienne. But he soon noticed and slowed his pace, taking her hand in his as he did so and laughing.

"I forget your legs are shorter than mine," he said. "A brisk walk is almost like running for you … I'll slow down."

So, at a more leisurely pace, they made for the outcrop of rocks. Breathing in the cool salty air with the slight wind from the sea chilling her was refreshing. The walking gave her no time for thoughts and anyway, she needed to remember to stay in the moment. That was what life was about, wasn't it?

For now, the moment was good. With no time for thinking. They were two people engrossed in a brisk walk on a lonely beach, with the goal to have a dinner at a café with a view over the sea of the setting sun.

Once they had reached the rocks, Vivienne looked for a dry one to sit on.

"Goodness, Vivienne," said Ivor, "you have real rosy cheeks." He bent down and softly kissed her. Vivienne, taken by surprise, nevertheless responded with passion, then laughed.

"Whew ... that is all my energy gone," she said. "I need to sit a few more minutes before we go on that brisk walk back."

Ivor also found a large dry rock to sit upon and for ten minutes or so, they rested, saying nothing, doing nothing, but listening to the never-ending swish of the waves breaking on the shore then rolling back to join the ocean. This wordless communication was one they both appreciated and it was at about the same time that Vivienne was thinking she was ready to walk back on the soft sea sand that Ivor said, "Ready, Vivienne? The café is calling."

He put out his hand to help pull Vivienne to her feet and then they were off on their walk back to the distant gate through which they had come.

By the time they had reached the car, the clouds in the sky were changing colour. A reddish tinge coloured them and clouds lay in ripples across the sky.

"The view's even better from the café," said Ivor, "as we are a bit higher ... there are a few steps to a raised covered verandah where it's great for a semi-outdoor meal."

Sitting at a table for two Vivienne said, "Ivor, you haven't mentioned painting at all this afternoon ... are you still a passionate artist?"

At that, he put out his hand and took hers. "Vivienne I am still a passionate artist, but I have found there is more to life than art... and painting..." He looked very serious as he said... "I found you. It sounds corny coming from a man of my age, but does it matter at what age one finds one has a heart that is full of love...that's what I have right now, Vivienne."

Vivienne, also not used to talking about her feelings, was touched by this man's outspokenness. She squeezed his hand and smiled as she looked at him. With that gesture, she was sure he would understand her feelings were the same.

The waiter had arrived with the menu, but as they were looking it, Ivor became aware of the setting sun.

"Look at the sky, Vivienne, look at the sky," he said, to the amusement of the waiter ... then to the waiter and to Vivienne, he said, "Do you mind coming back in a few minutes? We have come to see the sunset sky with its fiery red ripples and golden clouds..." The waiter smiled and nodded, and Vivienne turned her attention to the sky.

The colours were rich gold, deep red, rose pink and yellow ... in the form of ripples of clouds. And already the reds were fading and the navy of night was creeping into the scene.

"So rapidly it changes," said Ivor. He nodded to the waiter, who was still hovering. "We've seen the best of it," he said. "Thank you for your patience. Vivienne, my dear what would you like to drink? Please leave the menu with us for a few minutes."

The waiter nodded in agreement and went off to fetch the drinks whilst Vivienne and Ivor studied the menu.

"Now look at the sky, Vivienne, it's still beautiful, but we caught it at its very best," he said. Vivienne had one eye on the menu and one on the sky. She too was captured by the amazing cloud formation along with the now much softer shades of gold and red as night caught up with day ... and started to take over. The waiter was back with the drinks as Ivor asked Vivienne, "How is the menu. Vivienne?"

"Some lovely starters, Ivor, but I will just go for the main dish, thank you. The prawn curry is what I'll choose" She thought again of Henriette's disdain of Cape curries ... but that was before therapy, she thought with a smile.

Ivor was studying the menu as well. "I'd like something light," he said. "Maybe a salad with fish. And for dessert?"

"Crème brûlée is my choice," said Vivienne. "I can't make that at home and I do enjoy it."

"The same for me," said Ivor, and as the waiter went off to organize their food, they both sat back in their chairs to enjoy the sunset. And their togetherness. Their drinks arrived shortly and they smiled at one another and clinked glasses.

"This is a special day for us," said Ivor. "We haven't had the traditional honeymoon ..." He smiled at Vivienne "... so small day treats like this are going to take its place."

Vivienne was in total agreement. The food arrived shortly and both were quiet as they ate their main dish and dessert.

Vivienne was feeling sleepy and Ivor noticed it.

"You are tired, Vivienne," he said with concern. "That walk was challenging."

"Yes, Ivor, the sea air, the walk, the lovely dinner, and the sky … all perfect, but I'm ready for sleep now."

They thanked the staff, Ivor paid and tipped well, and they were soon walking back along the path to the car. Ivor left the sunroof up.

"It will be a bit windy now, Vivienne," he said, "and you may like to snooze as I drive."

Vivienne touched his arm in gratitude. "That sounds unsociable, but I would love to doze while you drive," she said, smiling at Ivor.

He nodded, and started the car and they were soon on the drive home …

Ivor kissed Vivienne goodbye the next morning. "It's unfortunate that I have to work most of the day when we have just got married, Vivienne, but I have to start working on four very large canvases for a commission to go on the Exhibition Centre's Entrepaneurial Day and I have a date by which I must finish.

Vivienne looked at him with a concerned expression. She gently stroked his face. "Ivor, you have a duty and this is your love, your painting. I am quite all right on my own.

I have you in afternoons and nights and on those days out … like yesterday. It was lovely and thank you."

Ivor relaxed and he smiled slightly. "Really."

"Yes, really Ivor. You'll make me happy if you make yourself happy." She hugged him, adding, "I'm fine on my own, Ivor, I really am. I'm used to it. Besides, I can't wait to see those big paintings that you are doing."

Ivor's expression changed from one of concern to relaxed and peaceful. "Yes, they are a challenge and I'm loving it. If you're sure?"

"Certainly, Ivor. Now off you go." She smiled as he picked up a bag of painting materials and waved goodbye to her.

Vivienne meant what she said. She was content with this new phase of life and somehow painting wasn't so important to her now. Her priority was to have a home Ivor loved coming back to, and food he enjoyed eating.

Life had been stressful of late, but now the stress was less. She had the day to do with whatever she wished. Evenings, now that the stress was over, were pleasant. She cooked for Ivor, and they took their time over the meal, enjoying a glass of wine with it. And then they retired to the lounge.

Ivor had got into the habit of asking Vivienne to sit next to him and she knew in this way he felt more secure about opening up to her.

For years he had been bottled up, but Lady Lavender's healing and cleansing had done wonders for him. There wasn't a lot he could tell her as his life had been strictly about art... art exhibitions, teaching art, experimenting with new techniques, and he didn't want to talk about art as much as he wanted Vivienne to talk about herself.

He asked lots of questions. And Vivienne enjoyed answering them. She never knew quite where the conversations would take them, but she was ready to talk about her time in a government school, at home in the country when she was married to Paul, about the girls' finishing school she had ended up at.

So she had at hand a tasty treat like crystallised melon when she spoke about her life and Ivor cautiously spoke about his feelings ... about never envying married people, because for him it was never going to happen .... Or so he thought. She knew as he drew her closer to him, that there was much he wanted to talk about when he was ready.

But, today, what was she to do? Perhaps a visit to Lady Lavender to thank her for officiating at their small wedding ceremony. She hadn't thanked her properly.

*What for lunch?* She had a great pineapple fish dish that she could make quickly when she returned, but, for now, she'd best be off as soon as she could.

Her house in order, she took her big sling bag and small sketch book and fine-liner pen … just in case … and soon was off down the front stairs and past the cafe… smiling at everyone as she walked. Then across the road, down the road a bit till she found the winding path going steeply downhill to Lady Lavender's old fisherman's cottage.

She still marvelled at its proximity to the waters of False Bay, yet its setting was with a background of mountains.

Down the last bit of path and right to see the familiar quaint cottage with its crooked chimney and big brass knocker.

She knocked, smiling as she did so.

In a very short while, the door opened, and there stood Lady Lavender, today in a sunshine-yellow long dress. Her dark eyes had brilliance about them and a sparkle too, as she said, "Do come in please, Vivienne. How good of you to call on me."

"Lady Lavender, it is me who has to thank you … it was so very kind of you to do such an extraordinary thing as to officiate at our small wedding. I wondered how you would ever get there with no road to your house."

"Ah, my dear lady, there is more to me than a pretty face." Vivienne smiled at this as no one would call Lady Lavender pretty... "But I have associates who connect deeply with me. And it was no trouble for one of them to take me across False Bay in his motor boat. A first for me, but most enjoyable."

"Really, Lady Lavender, you astonish me," said Vivienne. "I wondered how you got there, but you told me it was all under control so I didn't ask questions."

"Very wise, Vivienne... the old saying MIND YOUR OWN BUSINESS – MYOB, and how I got there and back was my business. From Rooi Els, I was driven to the venue where the nuptials took place. I did stay a short while at your reception then I was whisked back to the boat and brought back here. Thank you. It was a very different day for me."

Vivienne knew that Lady Lavender wouldn't want her to talk too much about what had happened. And she agreeably followed the mysterious woman into the kitchen. She had a feeling Lady Lavender wanted to talk to her and not about the wedding. So it was ginger tea and this time it was biscuits with a bite to them.

"Chilli?" she asked.

"Yes, a touch of chilli ... some other spices and the usual butter. Vivienne, I have been watching you and I am most pleased with your development. From the old Vivienne, so caught up with herself and her wants you have become a very nice person with a lovely energy. Keep it up, Vivienne. And Ivor will benefit from it as well."

Vivienne didn't reply as she just knew Lady Lavender didn't expect her to … instead, she took a bite of the spicy cookie. And laughed slightly. "Yes, it has a bite, Lady Lavender," she said. "But it's a tasty bite."

"Yes, meant to wake a person up," said Lady Lavender. "But I am pleased to see you are mostly awake. By the way. Vivienne, do you understand anything about energy?"

"No," said Vivienne. "I don't …"

"Well, we are moving into a new world. Now the world itself is still the same, but it is we who are different. We are to vibrate at a much higher level, to stay on this high level and on that plane, there is no room for negativities… the old feeling of hurt over small slights, or of negative thoughts or feelings about others. We are the forerunners and if we do our job properly, it's like osmosis … those around us will feel this new beautiful energy and they, too, will cast off old negative thoughts and ways …" She looked at Vivienne with gimlet eyes. "It is important to stay on a course that is right for you.

Only you can know that course, but I see you are remembering it's now, but it's not just you now, you have Ivor in your life and he needs special care. He is a fine man with also a beautiful energy, but due to earlier circumstances in his life, he has been stunted. His growth limited. And you, as a rich source of energy can provide him with a nurturing space to allow him to reach his full potential. Am I making sense to you, Vivienne?" she asked.

Vivienne, who had been silent whilst enjoying the biscuit and the ginger tea, had been listening and she nodded. "Yes, Lady Lavender, you are making sense to me. Just this morning I was wondering about my direction now and telling myself that Ivor has needs that were as important as my own and I needed to address and nurture these."

"Quite right, Vivienne," said Lady Lavender. "There are those of us in the universe, who have been handpicked as Light Givers, as leaders of others by our thoughts and actions, and in maintaining a high peaceful vibration ... I am one of them and amongst those I have chosen to train and develop is you. The path may not always be easy to follow, but you will be serving humanity in the best way you could."

Vivienne, used to Lady Lavender by now, nodded her head, but said nothing.

"Again, very wise , Vivienne," said Lady Lavender with a smile. "You are getting to understand me … I work on many dimensions and, at night, I work with the universal elements in helping to lead mankind into a better, kinder more loving way of living. And you will be doing the same, working with Ivor and those that he leads. It is important work, Vivienne. Artists do have a voice in society and as I said before, the energy they put into their paintings does affect those who see them or hang them on their walls."

Vivienne nodded. "Thank you. Lady Lavender, I will take care with my route."

"The big thing is to stay in the moment, Vivienne. You stray quite often I've noticed, letting your thoughts wander all over the place."

Vivienne winced slightly. This was true. She knew it was.

"It's so difficult, Lady Lavender," she said.

"Now, dear, don't whine. It doesn't suit you."

At this, Vivienne laughed.

"Everything, you experienced was the way it had to be, but that is in the past and you have dealt very well with it. Equally, the lessons you have had from me are meant to stay with you. Remember, stay in the moment, that's all you have, and remember thoughts are like wild horses, be gentle with them, just bring them back and centre yourself to get that peaceful no-thought head."

Vivienne decided to talk. "Lady Lavender, I knew I needed to come to you today ... but I thought it was for me to thank you again for what you did for us at our wedding."

"No, you didn't come for that, Vivienne. That is in the past and I don't need thanking ... you came for another lesson and, this time, it is to maintain a high level of energy and keep a peaceful no-thought head. Intuition will always guide you as to what you need to do next. There is a big difference between intuition and a busy chattering mindless head. I think you are recognizing the difference."

Vivienne nodded her head slowly. "Yes, I think I am, Lady Lavender. It is like a voice in my head telling me what to do. It isn't that chattering left brain."

"And one last thing," said Lady Lavender. "Should someone start telling you a lot of negative stuff, do not engage in the conversation. Say nothing. In this case, the negative input will go in one ear and out the other and leave you untouched. Should you involve yourself in the talk, you will bring down your vibrations. So a silent tongue please. Vivienne."

Vivienne nodded. *Yes, she understood.*

Then Lady Lavender added, "You are right ... it is intuition belonging to your higher self, the part of you that is to keep living on a high fine vibration. If you fall quickly lift yourself. Don't say in a low vibration. It's not for you."

Lady Lavender gave her a rare smile. Her smile had an energy and warmth about it that flooded Vivian, so that she felt uplifted.

From behind her chair came the big black cat. "Captain; she is a good friend now." And Lady Lavender looked with affection at her cat. She nodded. "He knows, he told me so."

"I will be watching over you, Vivienne, and will always be close. You and I have spent lifetimes together, which you do not remember, but I know you very well. You are special to me. And I will play an important part in helping you in this new world. A very beautiful one, Vivienne. You and I are lucky to be forerunners in the development of others."

The big black cat had come out and was squatting in front of Vivienne. She looked with respect at the cat. "Am I correct in thinking Captain says it's time for me to leave?"

"Perfectly right," said Lady Lavender. "You have done very well to understand my cat's language."

"Then I'll be off," said Vivienne. "It's been lovely to be with you." Then she remembered that Lady Lavender didn't like being thanked.

She saw a twinkle in the dark eyes of Lady Lavender. A little spark of light actually. And she smiled.

"I'll visit again," she said.

"You certainly will," said Lady Lavender, standing up and going with Vivienne to the door. "Everything is exactly as it should be. Nothing happens by chance."

With those words ringing in her ears, Vivienne made her way home.

# Chapter 2

Back in her kitchen it didn't take long for Vivienne to get out frozen filleted fish, dice it and cover it with cornflour mixed with soy sauce. Then arrange it in a casserole dish and cover with a sauce. This she made from pineapple juice flavoured with soy sauce and thickened with corn flour. A little sherry gave an extra-interesting flavour. All this was topped with pineapple chunks and it went into the oven to cook thoroughly before being decorated with pieces of green pepper. Vivienne also cooked rice and made a salad. She set the dining-room table and all was in readiness when Ivor came home.

Vivienne now was fully aware of being in the moment. She remembered, too, hearing that one must never laden a man just returning from work, whatever that might be, with an outpouring of the day's woes. Just be silent and let him unwind, she had heard.

So as he entered the kitchen, she hugged him, saying nothing. He had arrived with a fairly tense look on his face, but with Vivienne's warmth he had relaxed. Vivienne was glad when he returned the hug then said, "Let me take off my overcoat, Vivienne, then I will feel far more comfortable."

"Let me take it for you," said Vivienne as he disrobed.

"No, Vivienne, I like to hang it a certain way, and there's a hook behind your kitchen door. Thanks all the same."

Having hung up his coat, he breathed out deeply. "Wow, now I'm feeling light and airy … ready for lunch …" He smiled at Vivienne. "Do I smell something in the oven?"

Time to talk, thought Vivienne.

"Yes, Ivor, I hope you like it. It's one of my favourites – pineapple fish." Then she handed a dishcloth to Ivor and said, "Maybe you'd like to help and take it out of the oven and through to the dining room?"

"Certainly, my dear. With pleasure."

"Then let's go through to the dining room," said Vivienne.

Soon the pineapple fish was on the table and both were helping themselves to servings of it and of rice and salad.

Ivor had relaxed by now and put out his hand to hold Vivienne's. "Vivienne, how can I compare this with the couple of biscuits and some cheese I usually have for lunch. You are spoiling me."

Vivienne looked at Ivor. "Ivor it's my huge pleasure to find interesting dishes to cook for you. I love it… so we are both happy."

"I am particularly glad to be home as I struggled with my painting this morning. It simply didn't flow. But now I'd like to know how you spent your morning. Not doing housework, I hope?" He smiled at her.

"Oh no," said Vivienne. "I had a far more interesting day than that. I went to see Lady Lavender."

"You did? To thank her for officiating at our wedding?

"Well, that was my intention, but she had other things to talk about." Here, Vivienne hesitated. What Lady lavender had told her sounded really foolish. So she shrugged slightly and told him about the chilli biscuit and that Lady Lavender was pleased with her development.

"Oh, and so am I... you are becoming an excellent artist," said Ivor.

The subject having been changed, Vivienne picked up on it. "When is our next day out to paint?"

"Really Vivienne," Ivor laughed, "we've just been out."

"But we didn't paint," said Vivienne.

"True." said Ivor. "Then what about you let me see if I can finish one large canvas tomorrow and the day after we can go somewhere ...where would you like to go?"

"I'd like to see Julie and get her to paint with us," said Vivienne.

"You seem drawn to Rooi Els," said Ivor thoughtfully. "Perhaps I can invite one or two of my students as well. We do have to practice for this presentation we are to do in a few weeks' time. Would that suit you, Vivienne?"

Remembering Lady Lavender saying that Ivor, too, was starting to flower and grow in his own way, she agreed. "You invite any of them you like," she said, "and I'll see if Julie is available. It was her idea as well that you invited students to paint with us. I believe there are penguins there. I visited them at Boulders, but didn't try to sketch or paint them."

"Sounds good, Vivienne. You make plans and so will I ... we will set off early, at about 7.30 in the morning, as it will take more than an hour to get there."

Plans developing, Ivor retired to the bedroom to rest and Vivienne tidied the kitchen and thought of dinner.

The phone rang. It was Steven and she was happy to talk to him.

"Hello, Steven." she said, in a steady voice.

She and Steven knew each other so well and Steven immediately said,

"Hi, Mom, good to hear you and I know everything's okay by the sound of your voice."

Vivienne smiled into the phone. "You know me too well, Steven. Yes, it is all good, Steven. Thank you. I am on an even keel at the moment. Happy to be Ivor's wife."

She said this expecting a reaction from Steven, but surprisingly there was none. Instead, Steven said, "I knew you had years of life ahead of you and I'm glad you have found someone you enjoy." He hesitated and said with a small laugh, "You are so much your own person that I wondered how you would ever open up enough for a guy to get to know you, Mom."

"Really, Steven," Vivienne said, with mock indignation.

"But I guess you've changed, Mom. You are nice to Mariette and I know you mean it."

Vivienne sighed to herself. It had needed a change of heart, she thought, but instead said, "And how it the baby, Steven? What are you calling her?"

"We haven't yet decided," said Steven, "but she is so dainty and pretty I'd like a name of a flower."

Vivienne thought of a daffodil, but didn't say it. Instead, she said, "What flower, Steven. A rose perhaps?

"No, that's too ordinary," said Steven. "I have been thinking of one. There are many beautiful flowers…"

"Well, that gives your something to do," said Vivienne. "There's petunia and poppy.

"You are not being helpful, Mom," said Steven.

Vivienne laughed. It was nice to be a bit light-hearted with Steven. He had brought such heavy energy to her, or rather she had had a bad time with herself. It was good to know she was beyond interfering in Steven's life.

"We are talking of a wedding soon, Mom," said Steven. "And I'll really love to meet Ivor. He sounded like a strong self-assured person when he chatted to me that time when you were painting the windmill."

Vivienne was glad that Steven had that impression of Ivor.

"You will come over to Paris for it, won't you Mom?" Steven asked. "We will wait a couple of months until our little flower is settled in a routine. At present, she keeps Mariette awake a lot during the night so she is tired."

"Do you help with the baby?" Vivienne found herself asking.

"Oh yes, Mom, I change nappies and bath her sometimes. Mariette and I share everything as much as we can. I told you she was the girl I've been waiting for."

Vivienne found that she was happy for Steven and said in a light sincere voice, "I know Ivor will love to come with me to Paris. He once lived there as an artist and painted there. So it will be like a homecoming for him. And, of course, I will love to see my little grandchild and meet her other grandmother and grandfather." Vivienne was surprised to find she really did mean what she said, and by the sound of Steven's voice, he was grateful for Vivienne's support.

"Well, that's a burden off me," he said. "To know my mom and her husband will be with me when Mariette and I marry... And that you are pleased with everything."

"My son, I always wanted you to be happy, and it makes me glad you have found what you want in a woman, I really am, even if it has taken you off to another country. Ivor and I will be glad to be at your wedding, please tell Mariette's parents that ..." and with a bit more light chat about her own wedding, Vivienne rang off.

*What strides she had made!* She thought as she carefully put her cell phone away. An involuntary thought of Lady Lavender came into her mind. But she reminded herself not to let stray thoughts wander about in her head.

Ivor was sleeping. She realised he was under stress with all the changes in his life and still having a painting commission to do. Maybe he should be painting this afternoon and not sleeping. She worked at organizing a dish for dinner, whilst she waited for him to surface.

When he did, his hair was tousled and he rubbed his eyes sleepily. "That was a great sleep, thanks, Vivienne," he said.

"Is the painting stressing you," Vivienne asked, as she put her hands on his shoulders.

"How did you guess, my dearest wife?" he answered. "To tell you the truth, it is. I have to paint the seasons, spring, summer, autumn and winter. Anything I like, but they are big paintings. I struggled this morning with spring."

"What would you say if I suggested we go back to the studio now, and I come with you … to do nothing but be there … and you see if your inspiration is back? I have dinner prepared and have nothing planned for this afternoon."

Ivor glanced at his cell phone. "There is time, Vivienne. And thank you for the offer. I like it." A light and cheerful expression came onto his face. "Come. Dearest wife, the energies are back and let us go …" He smiled at her as he got up, went into the kitchen and retrieved his coat from the hook behind the kitchen door. "I know myself," he said, "and the block has gone. My creativity is back."

And taking Vivienne's arm, he led her out of the kitchen to the back door which she locked, then with Ivor leading the way they went down the flight of steps to his car.

Vivienne felt a lift of her spirits. She would not be painting. She would not be doing anything, but she would be there for Ivor.

As he drove, he said to Vivienne, "These are important paintings. They are part of the exhibition I will be doing in a few weeks' time. I have a free hand to do what I like, but this morning my creative spark was missing. I need to paint the glory of spring. The joy of the new buds on a tree, when suddenly all the trees have that faint green blush as if an artist had brushed them all over with a spring-green colour."

Ivor was smiling as he turned into his road and arrived outside his driveway gates. As he unlocked them remotely, he said to Vivienne, "Oh, I'm excited Vivienne. Thank you for the offer of coming here for me to paint. It was so insightful of you, and my creative spark is back."

"That's lovely, Ivor," said Vivienne quietly. She knew she would not be doing anything. But Ivor would be doing what he felt he was born to do … to inspire through his paintings.

It didn't take long for Ivor and Vivienne to enter the house. Vivienne could see that his pot plants had water around them so he had not forgotten to water them. And the lounge was as she knew it, full of framed paintings standing on easels. Ivor indicated to Vivienne to settle where she liked as he disappeared into the large room in which he painted.

Vivienne gave him time to organize himself then she showed herself at his door. He was mixing paint on his large palette, but he looked up at Vivienne. "You don't hinder my creativity,

Vivienne, and if you like you can stay in this room. In fact, I'm not quite ready to paint... I am doing a very creative painting, nothing precise but, at the same time, it must have the feeling of new beginnings, or the new birth that spring brings. I'm about to give birth, Vivienne." He smiled at her. "I imagine a scene of one very large and beautiful tree standing to one side with long fronds overhanging a still pool of water in a river. On the banks are bright-green shoots of new leaves pushing themselves out of the soil and some wild flowers. Cerise and mauve and yellow on the river bank. This old willow tree with long bare fronds that hang over the river show small green bumps where new leaves are sprouting, some already out, others about to become leaves. There is a soft green hill behind and a blue sky above. The fronds reflect in the river. It's all there, Vivienne."

Vivienne just smiled softly and nodded. She didn't want to interfere with his spurt of energy for painting. She found a comfortable chair and settled herself. In a matter of minutes Ivor had involved himself with mixing his paints and was then using his big brush, the hake, randomly putting on patches of paint. Vivienne held her breath ... *would what he was doing be the creative work he wanted to paint?* She decided not to interfere with his energy by having her own thoughts as she saw his brush dipping into various pools of paint on his palette, blobbing it on the watercolour paper then she watched as he cleaned his brush and wiped it on a cloth before immersing it in another colour.

She didn't like to look as to her it seemed patchy and rather a mess. So she turned her chair to gaze out of the window where a bird was tearing fronds off a palm tree she guessed in order to build its nest. Her attention now was on the bird, a bright-yellow bird. She didn't watch Ivor as he painted. Time went quickly and Vivienne sat quietly watching the bird. It had started a nest on a branch just outside the window with a few strands of grass and now it flew up and with its beak wove the strip of grass it had in its beak into the rough start of a nest.

The palm tree was a bit further away and she watched as it flew back to the palm tree, nipped at the base of a leaf, and then flew off, pulling a long strand of the palm leaf with him. Vivienne smiled. Building material, she thought, as the bird returned to the branch near the window. Now the bird deftly wove the new strip of leaf in with the strands already there, pulling it together to form the start of a nest. Off the busy little bird flew to get yet another strand of palm leaf to weave it in with what was already there. Vivienne watched as the nest took shape, then, all of a sudden, the bird flew off.

Tired, I guess, wants a rest, thought Vivienne. It was at much the same time that Ivor stopped for a break. He gently ruffled Vivienne's hair.

"Thank you, my dearest wife," he said. "This has turned my day around. I was feeling so disheartened when I came back to the house for lunch, but now I am happy. Have a look."

Vivienne swivelled herself around and drew in a deep breath. It was a very creative method of painting, blobs of paint, but though it was far from finished, he had caught the joy of a spring day, where new birth was bursting forth. The new leaves on the long swinging fronds overhanging a still pool of water, their reflections visible in it. On the banks beneath the old willow tree were patches of colour, of flowers bursting out of the earth. A blue sky with soft white clouds shone above the river scene. It wasn't finished, but it would entrance any viewer, thought Vivienne.

In her turn, she smiled at Ivor. "Yes, you've caught the joy of a new spring day, Ivor," she said, adding, "I'm so glad for you, Ivor."

"I'm glad for me too," said Ivor, with great relief in his voice. "This morning, I just couldn't get going."

"But I see you watered the plants."

"Yes, I did that as it helps me to get creative, but it didn't work this morning." He put his arms around Vivienne and she responded. "You bringing me back here was the magic, and thank you." He gently kissed her.

"I've been watching a weaver create his nest." said Vivienne. "I hope his wife likes it. He's taken a break as he's probably tired.

"I'll just do a bit more if its okay, Vivienne," said Ivor. "I still want to add some sparkle to the picture … maybe another half an hour. Maybe you'd like to make some coffee." He smiled. "Not like yours, but there is everything in the kitchen."

"Yes, and I know where you keep the almond cookies, so I'll make coffee for both of us," said Vivienne, getting up and going into the kitchen.

Soon the kettle was boiling, the cookies on a plate and milk and sugar in each cup. Vivienne and Ivor sat on the porch outside ... the day was darkening as the sun was setting, but for both Ivor and Vivienne, it had been an interesting day.

Vivienne was looking very serious.

"I'm going to tease you, Vivienne, until you relax and laugh," said Ivor.

"Oh, you don't have to do that, Ivor," said Vivienne. "I admit my mind was wandering a bit. But I'm back here," she said, looking at him and smiling.

"And what have you on your mind?" asked Ivor.

Vivienne took a deep breath. She had just had an 'aha' moment when Lady Lavender's advice had struck home. She knew she was a new person and had risen to a higher level, a finer vibration, and she didn't need to micro-manage Ivor. She just had to be this new person, relaxed and confident, and relate to Ivor naturally. And he would rise by himself to new levels. But she couldn't tell him that, and so she said, "I've been thinking about our painting trip, the one where I'll ask Julie and you'll invite one or two of your students to practice for that important presentation day."

"Oh, yes," said Ivor. "There are two of the men who were on the course that I'd like to ask... there is Curly. He's is a very slight man, with talent, but no self-confidence.

"And Walter. He is much more of a man about town, good-looking and with some talent, but I seem to think he has a burden of some kind. Maybe us doing a bit of painting by ourselves will help him to loosen up."

"That's excellent," said Vivienne. "Do you think they would be easily available?"

"Oh yes, Curly is retired and Walter has a shop and can take time off when he wants. They both took up painting to give them some purpose in life."

"First, then, I'll contact Julie. Tomorrow, you finish your spring painting."

"Yes then on the following day we can go on our painting trip."

"So, I'll ask Julie to join us … what is the plan? Painting? Where, what?"

"I've decided," said Ivor, "You'll like this. Rooi Els is our destination … there is a lovely natural reserve, or there is the sea and there are the penguins. And the rocky mountain itself. Maybe Julie will find the perfect spot for us to paint and relax and chat as we paint and crit each other's work. Does that sound too harsh? I usually don't crit my students, but we are working at developing stunning paintings."

"Thank you Ivor, I love the idea," said Vivienne in delight. "I'm excited and hope you'll crit me too."

"A good teacher doesn't crit his developing artists," said Ivor. "He leaves them to crit their own. It's getting dark, and it's time we made for home." He said this with that little smile into his beard and Vivienne knew he was telling her that her home was his home, and that this house of his was just his studio, which he would again visit tomorrow and Vivienne knew she would come with him.

"Let's tidy up and get back then," said Vivienne. "I'll get the cups and plates washed and you see your studio is left as you like it."

It wasn't long before they were on their way home. Back in her yellow-curtained kitchen, Vivienne soon had her dinner dish warmed and ready to eat in the dining room. This night, however, Vivienne was thoughtful.

"Do you mind, Ivor, if I spend a bit of time chatting to Julie? She may have some ideas of where it would be good to meet and paint."

"Excellent and I'll call Curly and Walter," said Ivor.

Julie was delighted to hear Vivienne's voice. "And so soon after your wedding," she said.

"There's no honeymoon for us," said Vivienne. "Ivor has big paintings to complete for a commission, but we are taking a day or two a week to go out and enjoy painting somewhere. Ivor has a big presentation to do in a few weeks' time and I wondered if you would like to join us on our next painting day?"

"Oh yes, I'd love that," said Julie.

"But Ivor will be asking a couple of his students from the course. He had the same idea as you had."

"Not Maureen, I hope," said Julie with a laugh.

Vivienne laughed too. "No. fortunately, she's a thing of the past, but he has two of his men students he'd like to develop. One is called Curly – let's see how curly his hair is!" They both laughed. "The other is Walter. It sounds as if Walter takes himself too seriously, but has some talent as a watercolour artist."

"This sounds perfect," said Julie, "Where do you aim to do this outing?"

"We thought in Rooi Els, the day after tomorrow."

"Wonderful," said Julie, "and you could use my venue for the training. I have big grounds that run down to the sea as you know and what is more, I have a tea garden where we could get refreshments and also sit and chat… if the course allows that," she added.

"Oh, yes, it does," said Vivienne. "Ivor wants the artists to paint and he will crit us … not harshly, but just give pointers to develop better masterpieces." She smiled as she said this.

"Oh I'm delighted," said Julie. "I will get our cook to work some extra nice dishes for us for tea and lunch so don't bring anything with you to eat."

Vivienne was relaxed and happy as she ended her phone call. She looked at Ivor. He was in the lounge looking out through the stained-glass window at the darkening night sky. She went and stood next to him as he ended his second call.

"All in order," he said. "Curly has a motor bike and will get himself there and Walter will be dropped off … he didn't say by whom and I must say he sounded a bit mysterious…. We have two gentlemen artists who need our nurturing, Vivienne," said Ivor, turning to gently hold Vivienne's shoulders. "And we leave at seven-thirty day on the day after tomorrow, after I've finished my spring painting," he said. "It takes just over an hour to drive to Rooi Els."

Ivor and Vivienne turned and looked at one another. Ivor had his twinkle back in his eye and Vivienne had a relaxed smile.

"It's going to be fun, Ivor," she said, "and thank you for giving us the time." She stretched up and kissed him. She watched the genuine expression of surprise and then joy cross his face. Yes, he was growing as a person…

# Chapter 3

The next day Ivor chatted to Vivienne as they drove to his studio. Ivor worked on his spring painting, while Vivienne sat watching the little yellow weaver bird continue to build his nest. He had made great strides and the nest was looking almost ready to occupy. *I hope your wife will like it!*

Ivor was busy with his painting and Vivienne was fascinated to see the female bird return to inspect the nest. Her heart missed a few beats, as she saw the wife, not only inspect the nest, but tear it to pieces with her disapproving beak. Bits of dried palm leaf floated down as the indignant female bird flew off, leaving a dejected father bird behind.

But he was undeterred and Vivienne was pleased to see him start again, this time choosing two twigs to pull together to signal the start of a new nest.

Time went on and she was jolted into being aware of Ivor and his painting when he suddenly spoke. "Vivienne, it's been a magical morning, and I'm happy with what I've done. Look at the sparkle on that water. And the reflections of the almost leafless long strands of branch. And look how the sun lights up one side of the tree."

Vivienne turned from the window and got up to inspect Ivor's painting. Yes, he had captured the joy of a spring day with new leaves and little flowers, making her smile.

"It's lovely, Ivor," she said. "Is it finished?"

She thought perhaps she shouldn't have asked that, but Ivor fondly tousled her hair.

"What a thing to ask me," he said, in a light and happy voice. "Stop before you think it's finished, my old artist trainer told me, and when I look later, I will realise I stopped at the exact right time. I'm in love with it Vivienne," he said. "And it's good, because I can come back after our trip tomorrow to paint summer with an unburdened mind." He turned to Vivienne, "Let me clean up as quickly as I can and then let's go home… we have to think about tomorrow and, of course, eat lunch."

"Actually, no, as Julie said she would do that."

"Wonderful," said Ivor. "Who else could get so lucky?"

They were soon home and once lunch was over, Ivor invited Vivienne to share with him ideas on how to run the art training the next day.

"Do you think each artist should find his own spot to paint in … and we have an hour and a half to do this … then we can gather in Julie's tea garden and look at what each of you have painted. With some input on what might improve the work if it needs improving. Then we can have lunch and perhaps do another hour's painting. I'll pack paints and paper for us all," said Ivor. "And water, yes and water and cloths."

"That sounds perfect, Ivor," said Vivienne.

The next day saw Vivienne and Ivor driving along the coastal road next to the sea. It was always breath-taking. Beautiful blue sea and white waves, rocks, and mountains until they reached Rooi Els and found the short private road to Julie's studio.

They arrived just as a large motor bike turned in with a small man on it, a small man with a bald head. Ivor looked at Vivienne and smiled.

"That's Curly," he said.

"Really?" asked Vivienne. "I don't remember seeing him at your class."

"He was wearing a beret most of the time. But, today, he is Curly at his best."

He cheerily greeted the slim, middle-aged man with the bald head, "Curly, how are you?"

In a surprisingly deep voice, Curly replied, "So looking forward to this day of painting, Ivor. I haven't done much since the training, so this will be a refresher."

"Yes, get ready to be on exhibition in a couple of weeks' time. You and Walter, when he arrives, are my two best creative artists."

As he spoke a stylish car with a pretty young woman at the wheel drew into the park area. Ivor peered at the passenger.

"Ah, Walter," he said.

He waited whilst Walter leant over to kiss the young woman then to get out of the car. The car pulled off rapidly and Walter walked over to join the group.

Walter seemed in a hurry to talk and said, "Thank you for the invitation, Ivor. I appreciate the chance to practice."

No one asked Walter if that was his wife... but Vivienne had a feeling that it wasn't. Then she remembered Lady Lavender's instruction MYOB.

The group, after greeting one another, walked towards Julie's studio. The door was closed as the studio was only open on weekends, but, as they neared it, the door opened and there was Julie with her long golden hair and blue eyes. To think I thought she was a mermaid, thought Vivienne. But she could be one.

Julie was ecstatic to see them and hugged Vivienne and Ivor. And stood respectfully to be introduced to Curly and Walter.

"We have everything here," Julie said. "Look at the mountain behind us ..." and she pointed at the strange-shaped reddish rocky mountain, "and the sea in front ... wild flowers and Heather and Proteas and birds, of course. Sometimes, even penguins come ashore on our bit of beach below," she told them.

Vivienne perked up. "Penguins were what I was hoping for," she said.

"It's rare, but it does happen. Come let us go through to the back garden ..." She led them through her studio with its array of framed photographs mostly in black and white, "...because it's more dramatic," she said.

And through the kitchen door to the garden outside where there were tables with umbrellas…and a beautiful view of the sea from the back garden with the small twisty path that led down to the beach.

"So you can take your pick of what you want to paint and where," said Ivor. "I have paper, paints, palettes and water for all of you. The paper is already on a board so it will not rumple and will stay firm … rest it on a rock or anything you like. Just wander about first to see what catches your fancy then make yourself comfortable. I also bought some small folding stools so you can sit to paint."

"Marvellous," said Vivienne. She looked at the two men. Curly looked nervous and Walter looked distracted. Would they paint their best …? They needed to unwind, to relax, she thought. But maybe just being here would be all they needed.

Curly spoke first in quite a deep voice. "Thank you Ivor sir," he said. "I'm not sure of myself."

Ivor looked at him and nodded. "Know that you have all the knowledge within, Curly," said Ivor, "and just relax… go and walk about. It's all fenced and safe… and wherever you feel comfortable, settle there. Just breathe and imbibe the atmosphere, draw in what you can… plants, birds, the sky, the mountains. You and they are all connected and when you feel a spurt of energy, a connection, you could call it, just open your eyes and arrange some paints on your palette. Keep the water handy so you can brush it onto the paper… let the colours mix on the paper."

Curly had visibly relaxed. He had big pale-blue eyes and sandy eyelashes. His face was thin and pale. Related to his bald head, thought Vivienne, then regretted thinking that.

Curly was talking. He had taken a big deep breath and had a small smile on his face. "Thanks, Ivor, sir, I like that."

"Yes," said Ivor, "and in an hour and a half's time please make your way back to this covered tea garden with what you have painted. And let me have a look at it. So, you are ready? Here is the bag of art materials you may be needing."

Curly nodded agreeably and took the bag from Ivor. Soon, he was wandering down the path towards the sea and the beach. Ivor watched him, and then smiled.

"He's ok," he said. "He will find his way. And now you, Walter?"

He spoke to Walter, well-built and nice-looking with brown eyes and dark hair. His slightly stressed expression had relaxed. He looked expectantly at Ivor. "I haven't practiced much since our course," he admitted. "I'm unsure of myself."

"It will all come back," said Ivor, walking towards Walter and holding the bag of art materials. "You heard what I said to Curly. The same applies to you. The paper is on a board so you can rest it against something like a rock or a tree branch when you paint ... and everything else you need is in this bag. Like Curly, check what interests you... a walk amidst the heathers and greenery, the large rocks, the mountain behind, the view below or an actual walk to the beach where there is the sea with small waves and sprays of water where the waves break. Not to mention the sky above."

Walter nodded. He, too, had relaxed slightly. "I'll just wander around up here amongst the shrubs and trees," he said.

"Don't forget to paint," said Ivor with a smile. He was looking directly at Walter, who flinched slightly.

"No, I won't," he said. "I will paint something even if it isn't very good."

"Now we don't want that kind of talk," said Ivor. "It will all be good because you have the knowledge and are in a marvellously creative place here. Now off you go and I'll see you back here in an hour and a half."

Julie and Vivienne were standing together, listening to Ivor and watching the men. "So, we do the same?" asked Julie.

"Yes," said Ivor. "Exactly the same". He smiled as he handed Julie an A4 sheet of watercolour paper already steadied on a light board. He handed her a bag of painting equipment. She nodded and walked off down a small path that Vivienne hadn't noticed before.

"It also leads to the beach," Julie said softly, "but to a different part so I won't bump into Curly."

"And Vivienne. You … last but certainly not least…" Ivor handed her a bag of art materials.

"You know, I think I'll just stay up here," said Vivienne, "and paint the mountain. It's nicely visible from this outside eating area."

"Why not," said Ivor. "I'll also be staying up here. Maybe I'll sketch a bit myself. This is all so creative, so much calling to be drawn."

Vivienne looked at Ivor. He was watching as Walter wandered rather aimlessly about.

"I'm a bit concerned about Walter," said Ivor. "He has talent, but his mind isn't here today. I'm not sure where it is, but wandering up here amongst the heaths and wild flowers and shrubs may settle him."

"Yes," said Vivienne, "by just walking around in a so-called aimless manner, that creative spark may burn in him. It did for me when I wandered about last time."

Ivor looked at her. "That's the way one gets creative," he said. "By idly doing nothing. It doesn't always work. I hope it does for Walter."

The land up here was fairly flat and they could see the tall frame of Walter wandering around.

Vivienne looked at Ivor. "No, I'm not going after him," said Ivor. "He will paint or he will not. We will see."

"But don't let me hinder you," he said, smiling at Vivienne.

"Oh no," said Vivienne. "I'll also wander about a bit to stir up my creative juices."

She nodded to Ivor, then went off with her bag of art materials and her paper on a board. She wandered among the rocks and green plants. She could nicely see the mountain from where she was and decided this was to be her focal point. The reddish mountain leaning sideways. She squinted at it. She wasn't going to paint it as something precise. She decided to play with the paint and with the energy of the mountain. *Who knew what would turn up on her board?*

She found a nice low branch to settle herself on. The water jar she perched on another short thick branch and the palette she laid on her knees. It was all rather awkward, but she had managed her balancing act. The board she also perched on a slight protruding branch. It was at an angle which meant the water flowed easily down. What to start with? The sky above or the mountain? She squinted at the mountain. The mountain she thought, and it drew her towards it, so that her energy and that of the mountain mingled. How exciting, she thought, as she rapidly splodged a reddish-brown paint onto the middle of the paper, then using her brush, inclined it sideways resembling the mountain that looked as if it would fall over at any time.

She smiled at the thought. No, it wasn't falling over, it was energizing her. She added a touch of brown, left some white patches, and let the paint mingle in its own way. She rather liked the result. Nothing like the mountain, just her feeling of the mountain. Then she blobbed in some blue sky with white clouds, and around the mountain, she dropped in green paint to indicate the greenery that surrounded the mountain.

She found herself in another world. That of the energies of the sky, the land and the mountain. A sort of magical place and she smiled … how odd to be sitting on a tree branch, holding her board with its piece of A4 paper in its firm position with her water on one branch, her palette on her knees and yet, somehow, she and the tree were in harmony. It was a lovely feeling. Nothing strange at all.

Time went quickly and she noticed her time was up. Time to be going back to the tea garden and Ivor. She wondered if Walter had settled in the end.

Back at the tea garden she saw Julie back with a bright painting of blue water, pale sand and dark rocks. And Curly back with a very different rendering of a similar scene. His was very loose and creative, leaving a lot to the imagination. She recognized it as the way Ivor had taught them and she liked what she saw.

And then along came Walter. He had drawn some shapes that could be rocks and indicated some shrubs, but he hadn't put any paint onto what he had sketched. He shook his head. "I'll join you next time you have a session," he said, in a low voice. "I'm not in a good place today." He placed the bag of painting materials on the table.

Ivor nodded, indicating that he understood.

At that moment, through the dining room door, came the young woman who had dropped Walter off in the morning. She looked slightly agitated as she said to Walter in a low voice.

"Can you come now, Walter? Your wife knows and it's best you get home." She took his arm and Walter nodded to the group and to Ivor. "I'm sorry. Ivor. I'll ring and explain to you later." And he let the young woman lead him out through the dining room to her car outside. Soon, they heard it start up and leave.

No one said anything. Ivor just shook his head. "I'll be taking a look at what you have painted. Mostly to see you have included dark shapes and objects that show up your points of interest. A dark shadow, a dark tree trunk, a dark rock can all play their part.

"I am not expecting photographic reproductions, but rather, the colours and the energies of the place on paper are what we want. Something that fascinates and draws people's attention. If there is a lot of white space it's very important, like Curly has done." He pointed to Curly's interpretation of the beach sand, the rocks and the waves, all simplified, with lots of white space left.

"You must admit this has charm," he said. The group all agreed. Ivor continued with his crits. "Nothing of importance goes dead centre. Shift it to one side or the other. Make the eye focus on what you feel your painting is about. Every painting needs to have just one central message and dark shadows and objects can bring focus to that. The central theme. I don't want to get too academic. I like my artists to relax and to be creative and bring the audience into the picture through their rapture with what you paint. Don't try to be formalized. Just relax and have fun ... Curly, for instance, has done a lot to capture the eye."

The artists all looked at Curly's painting.

"Well done, Curly," said Ivor, sincerely praising the little man. "A great painting with lots of white spaces. Just close your eyes and look at it. You can sense the power of that curling wave as it crashes down and the serenity of the place."

His straightening shoulders told Vivienne Curly was appreciating himself. Vivienne saw a light come into Curly's eyes and she felt he had grown several inches. She smiled to herself. This is what Ivor was meant to do. To grow people. To show them they had talent when it was obvious to others if not to themselves.

"Thank you, Ivor, sir," said Curly. "I was honoured when you asked me to join this group. I am not a confident artist."

"You have amazing talent, Curly, and with just another session like this, you will be ready to work in front of people at the exhibition we are to be part of, now just weeks away." Ivor patted Curly on the shoulder, smiling at him as he did. Curly looked really happy with himself.

That was a success, thought Vivienne.

Julie's painting was in a very different style. It aimed at getting precise details of a scene and would appeal to a certain type of buyer.

"It's lovely Julie," said Ivor sincerely. "Very realistic. I can sense the power of that water as it crashes onto those rocks. Nice work, Julie."

Julie smiled. "I would never have painted that without you being here," she said. "So thank you for inviting me."

"And thanks for the venue and the lunch we are all looking forward to," said Ivor. "It has been great so far. Now let's see Vivienne's work."

He walked round to look at Vivienne's painting. He paused for quite a long time. Vivienne held her breath. She had so enjoyed doing that painting … but it didn't look like the mountain she knew.

But Ivor was serious as he said, "I like it, Vivienne. You've caught the majesty and mystery of this mountain. How many tales could it tell? Your painting has an energy about it that lifts me up so that I feel as if I was in that rock or very close to it… agreed it doesn't look exactly like the mountain," and he smiled as he said that … anyone could see Vivienne's painting and the mountain itself did not look the same, "but it's the feeling we get that is important. The feeling of the energy of this age-old rock sharing with us its feeling that everything in the world is as it should be. Yes, Vivienne you can be proud of what you have painted today."

All were happy with their work. Then Julie said, "I wonder how Walter is faring." The group looked at one another, but no one spoke until Ivor said, "I'm sure he's worked out whatever he needed to .. and he did say he will update me tonight. I will see if he will join our next and last session. Walter has talent. Today wasn't his best day though."

Julie spoke up, "Ivor, can we break for a bite to eat …. My stomach is rumbling."

"Why not?" said Ivor. "Good idea, Julie."

"There are just pizzas of different flavours," said Julie. "In case any of you are vegetarians, there is a pineapple cheese pizza. The others are chicken, ham and cheese, and spicy beef. ..."

They proceeded to order their choice of pizza.

"Thank you so much, Julie." said Ivor.

"There's a choice of things to drink. Milkshakes, cool drinks, even a light wine ..." Julie pushed her long golden hair out of the way. She indicated a drinks card. "My pleasure," she said. "Please just order and Maxine will bring them to you. John will be along with the pizzas in a short while. Shall we enjoy a lunch break then continue with the critting. It will be easier to concentrate," she said laughing, her blue eyes crinkling as she laughed.

She really is like a mermaid, thought Vivienne.

Soon the group were enjoying their lunch break with milkshakes and cool drinks and wine.

"Walter will be at our next session," said Ivor with confidence. "I'm sure the painting will help him."

They left it at that.

"We are not doing more painting," said Ivor, "not this afternoon. You have all done very well. Now we fill our buckets and just enjoy the rest of our time here.... Thanks, Julie."

"My pleasure," she said.

"What about walking as a group down to the beach? It is so refreshing."

"Yes, good idea," said Ivor. "That's what I need, salt air and sea water. Please lead the way, Julie, if all are agreed."

All were agreed. With Julie leading the way, her long golden hair swinging as she walked, they followed down the narrow path that Curly had taken. It was always a surprise to move behind the rocks and grass to get a sudden view of the sea, with its incessant sound of waves breaking on the shore and washing back. The group were about to split up and go in different directions when Julie whispered, "Look, Vivienne, there's a penguin."

To Vivienne's delight there was a penguin with its black coat and white vest, sitting on top of a rock. This penguin was not concerned with the arrival of a small group of artists and continued sitting on top of the rock.

"Oh, for a quick sketch," murmured Vivienne, getting out her sketch book and pen. The penguin seemed to know that it was required to sit still for a modelling session, whilst Vivienne did a quick sketch of it. She breathed a sigh of relief. "That has made my day."

The penguin continued sitting on the rock as the artists chatted and moved around. Ivor stood watching and Vivienne was still engaged in studying the penguin that at last got bored and hopped down and in an ungainly manner made for the sea where it was soon enjoying a swim.

"All that is so special," said Vivienne, with her eyes fixed on the penguin. It ducked and dived, and then soon was swimming out to sea. Vivienne turned to Ivor, who was watching Vivienne and the penguin. He smiled as she slipped her hand into his.

"I don't know what is about penguins that intrigues me so much," she said looking up at Ivor.

He had that little smile that disappeared into his beard and his hazel eyes were twinkling.

"You are so special, Vivienne," he said. "Your enthusiasm for life is so contagious. I even feel the thrill you felt on seeing a penguin."

Vivienne smiled as he squeezed her hand. The group wandered around on the beach, feeling the soft white sand and taking off their shoes, paddling in the icy sea.

"It's freezing," said Curly, but he was smiling.

Vivienne thought he looked a lot more sure of himself now than he had this morning. Some shell collecting, some laughing, as the occasional big wave splashed over them, and the rapport in the group grew.

Ivor had a satisfied look on his face and Vivienne knew for him this day had been a success. For her, too, it had been great to get out and, though it had ended up with a group out painting, instead of just her and Ivor, there was a satisfaction in knowing all had benefitted.

Over the sound of the breaking waves, Ivor said, "Okay, folks, time to be going back now. It's been a wonderful day all round, and let's all thank Julie."

More laughter and clapping then the group turned and headed for the studio and the carpark and soon they were all off, with Curly's motorbike sending out clouds of smoke.

"All good," he called as he drove off.

"Yes," said Ivor. "All good and thanks again, Julie ..."

The drive home was just as beautiful as the drive down. This time the roof of the car was off and Vivienne had her head back and was enjoying the wind in her hair. She wasn't thinking much at all and was surprised when Ivor said, "I have a feeling Walter will phone this evening."

They had barely got home when Ivor's phone rang.

It was Walter – Walter who wanted to talk.

"Ivor, I'm so sorry about this morning. And the drama and I'm sure you heard and am equally sure you guessed what is happening. That is Rose and I am involved with her." He stopped for breath. "She is much younger than I am, and very different from my current wife. I'm not sure where my life is going.

"My wife found out about Rose today so I had to tell her. I may be heading for a divorce from her. Luckily, we have no children, though we have been married for a long time." He stopped for breath, seeming to want Ivor to say something, but Ivor remained quiet.

Walter seemed to be thinking as he spoke. "My current wife and I simply live in the same house. We have no common interests, no conversation. And we fight a lot. I'm not a happy person." Then he added, "I took the painting course as a distraction. I thought it might clear my head. And that I could be satisfied with the life I have with the painting in it, but that was not so. My current wife is a controller, and she was jealous of the small bit of talent I showed."

"Not small, Walter," said Ivor. "You have a lot of talent, but you are not free in yourself to paint."

"That is so true," said Walter. "I feel shackled, manacled. Because my wife is also a critic and she didn't like your loose creative way of painting. She wants me to do a kind of photographic painting, very realistic. I like your approach, Ivor, but today, I wasn't able to concentrate. On our way to Julie's, Rose told me that my wife had been peeping through our lace curtains and saw her pick me up. I was jittery, too, sensing something was not going well and all hell broke out when I got home. She has thrown me out of the house. Locked it, and I don't have a key."

"So what are you going to do?" asked Ivor.

"I'm booking a room at a hotel," said Walter, "not for Rose to visit, but for me to get some peace and think things out. Divorce will be problematic, because my wife is not going to give me one. But she will make it very unpleasant for me if or when I go back."

His voice had a silent appeal. Ivor looked at Vivienne. "Yes, Walter, settle yourself somewhere on your own, and get some rest if you can. I do suggest that you come to my studio tomorrow and do some painting. You can talk to me, whilst you paint and maybe some of your turmoil will quieten down."

Walter's voice still held a sense of desperation.

"I don't think I'll sleep at all tonight," said Walter. "This has been a terrible day. It is fortunate or unfortunate that my maid knows Rose and likes her. And when my wife saw Rose pick me up, she got in a frenzy. So the maid phoned Rose, which is why she came back to take me home. To meet with a frenzied woman and the storm of the age. No, it's not been a good day and I don't know where I'm headed."

"Well, get to your hotel, Walter, take my address and get a taxi to drop you off say at nine tomorrow morning. We'll explore various techniques. My exhibition is a couple of weeks away and you are one person I selected to be on show as it were."

In his mind, Ivor could see Walter shaking his head.

"I'll never be able to do that," Walter said. "I'm too distraught."

"Eat and rest, Walter," said Ivor, "and I'll see you at nine tomorrow morning. Thank you for calling."

He rang off.

Vivienne was watching him. "Nice work Ivor, perfect answer for Walter. Painting will calm him and might even help him see in which direction he needs to go."

Ivor smiled at her. "How well you put it, Vivienne. That's what I hope happens for him. I'm glad he phoned."

And Vivienne said, "I'm glad you made the suggestion that you did. Let's have an early night shall we, then be ready for whatever tomorrow brings..."

# Chapter 4

The next day saw Ivor and Vivienne at Ivor's studio a good half an hour before Walter was expected. Ivor went into his studio, whilst Vivienne went into the kitchen to organize some refreshments for them all. Ivor cleared a space on a large work table next to his. He would be working on his large painting of summer and had told Vivienne he already had some idea of what he would be painting.

Vivienne, who had finished in the kitchen, joined him as he was organizing a space for Walter.

"Today, I'm painting summer," he said, "and in my mind there is that old willow tree that is hanging over the river, with its full splendour of delicate green leaves on wispy flying branches. I'd like to paint it on the right side my paper, as if the same tree in my spring painting is in it, but on the opposite side … so the pool of water you saw is not there now, as now the scene is one of rolling green grassy fields with distant mauvish mountains. The summer day is sunny and warm, hot, in fact and maybe there will be a little lamb resting under the tree and, in the distance, some horses in the fields. I'm not sure if this will work as a picture. Or if there needs to be something of more interest."

"What about an old hut? I remember you took me to draw one some months ago," said Vivienne.

"You are right, Vivienne. An old slatted wooden hut will add interest to the painting. I'll see how it develops. I may go off at a tangent." He turned and smiled that slow smile of his.

Vivienne responded in delight. "Of course, you might, Ivor. It is, after all, creative watercolour painting and I know you don't know what you are going to paint."

Vivienne noticed the secret smile he had… that was when he was at his most creative. She was glad. He was halfway to getting a good picture painted.

Ivor had set out a palette, paints, water, a cloth and a sheet of water-colour paper for Walter to paint on. His student's painting spot was ready.

"Walter is not going to distract you, is he?" asked Vivienne.

"No, Vivienne, I'll let him talk and get started first and when he's involved with the paint and no longer wants to talk, I'll paint. When I start it will all happen quickly so I'm not worried. I'm more concerned that Walter clears some of his mental burdens and lightens up."

"I guess in his position it's not easy to be light," said Vivienne. She could just imagine the angry wife and Walter's desperation.

"Well, let's not talk about it, or think about it," said Ivor. "Let's wait for Walter. I'm sure he'll be here and on time."

And just as Ivor had expected, at exactly nine am, a white taxi stopped outside Ivor's small wooden gate and Walter got out. He was wearing the same clothes he'd had on the previous day and, of course, he had not had a chance to go home and get a change of clothes.

Walter looked tired. He had dark rings under his eyes and his usual confident walk with shoulders thrown back was missing. It could be a heavy day, thought Vivienne as he rather dejectedly came into the lounge. His immediate reaction, however, was to stand and stare at all the framed paintings in Ivor's lounge.

He shook his head. "So much energy in all these paintings," he said. "That's what I don't have right now. Energy. Any energy at all."

"Come right in," said Ivor, "and come through to my studio where you and I will be working." He led Walter through the door to his studio where a large sheet of watercolour painting was waiting for him to work on and next to him was the place he had laid out for Walter.

Walter was looking around and Vivienne saw a distinct transformation. The sight of the paints and paintings had shifted his mind-set. He straightened up, but said, "I'm not ready to paint Ivor. I need to talk first. To unwind as it were."

"Right, let's get some coffee and find somewhere to sit. It's better if we sit here, because just now you will suddenly want to paint and everything is ready for you, as you can see. Take a seat," said Ivor. "There are chairs here. I sometimes like to sit and look outside. Vivienne was watching a bird make its nest, the other day.. It's good to distract oneself from random thoughts and get into the present moment. Which is you, here, with Vivienne and me."

Vivienne went to the kitchen. "Won't be long," she called.

Vivienne was soon back with a tray of coffee for all of them. "Please help yourself, milk and sugar, if you wish," said Ivor. "Then we can talk."

Walter took the coffee, added milk and sugar and seemed to want to take his time before talking.

Ivor waited.

At last Walter said, "This thing with Rose just happened. I wasn't looking for an affair or another wife. Or a girlfriend. But Rose came into my small hardware shop, looking for glue to fix a small table of hers. She was so friendly and also so totally useless at what I knew she had to do to get that table fixed that I offered to do it for her at no charge and to take it round to her flat.

"We got on so well. I felt I had known her forever, and we started meeting for lunch. Then besides the feeling of comradeship that we had, other feelings started to develop and I realized I was falling in love with her. Nothing I intended. And I hadn't thought of the consequences. Of Cecile, my wife, finding out. But she did. Of course, Rose feels bad, but she, too, has feelings for me. In fact, we are in love and it was such a lovely feeling. That combined with the painting was making my life worthwhile."

He stopped to sip at his coffee. Then continued. "I guess I need to just take one day at a time and face the music back with Cecile, if she will let me in the house."

"And Rose?"

"No, I will not stop seeing Rose," said Walter firmly.

"Well, you have made one decision," said Ivor. "When you are ready to paint please tell me and I'll suggest that you just paint your feelings today. It doesn't matter what it looks like. It's how you feel that needs to go on that paper."

Walter looked at him and actually smiled. "It's likely to be a lot of red for anger, and dark colours for gloom, and then maybe some bright yellow as the sun breaks through."

"I like the idea," said Ivor.

"Thanks Ivor, and when I've finished this coffee, I'm ready to paint."

Ivor looked at Vivienne, and they exchanged knowing glances. Ivor was moving along the path he was meant to and probably Walter was as well.

It wasn't long before all three of them were silently engaged in their own occupations, Vivienne in watching the weaver bird whose wife was approving of the next nest her hard-working spouse had made.

Ivor in painting summer, sploshed and dropped paint onto his board in a seemingly random way, and Walter, with deep concentration, painted a very colourful picture of how he felt.

All were engaged for the best part of an hour. Then all of a sudden all were finished, momentarily, and ready to talk.

Walter was smiling. "I feel marvellous," he said. "Look at my feelings. They are all over the place, but also there's a glimmer of light. I'll go home and face Cecile. Talk to her honestly about what our relationship is like and how I feel ..."

"Take it in slow motion," said Ivor "... don't rush it."

"The pace will depend on Cecile," he said with a wry smile. "She may throw things at me or kick me out of the house. But I love Rose and, really, Cecile and I don't have a marriage. Not at all ..."

For Ivor it had been a successful day as well. The big willow tree with the wispy hanging branches was nicely covered with small green leaves, the distant fields were a soft green and there was this rustic wooden hut that caught the eye and intrigued it. Some patches of bright wild flowers and sunlight shafting through the leaves and onto the old shed gave warmth to the painting.

"It's the painting exhibition soon," Ivor said. "This picture will be on it."

Walter hesitated then threw his shoulders back and said firmly, "Yes I will be there."

And Vivienne knew he would.

"I have some rough water to paddle through before then," Walter said wryly, "but I will weather it..."

Ivor nodded. "And if you get the chance, do some practice painting before we meet again."

Walter was tidying up his paints and picked up the painting he had done. "Do you mind if I take this with me?" he asked, then added, "I might even show it to Cecile, but she will probably get terribly angry. Who knows ...?"

Vivienne tidied up the coffee things and they were all ready to leave. Walter's taxi arrived, and Vivienne and Ivor set off in Ivor's dark blue sports car. Vivienne didn't say much, but was studying Ivor as he drove.

"I know you are looking at me, Vivienne," he said with a slight smile. "Did I measure up, dear one?"

"Most certainly, you did, Ivor," replied Vivienne in a light tone. "Walter is in charge of himself now. And he's logical and reasonable, not all over the place with wild emotion. He will work things out. Nice work, dearest one."

And she watched with pleasure as Ivor smiled that little smile of his that showed he'd had a satisfactory morning.

The next few days went smoothly. Ivor finished his "summer" painting and started on "autumn" with golden leaves and shafts of sunlight gleaming through trees that were dropping their leaves.

Steven phoned from Paris – he and Mariette had agreed on a name for the baby – Violet. The wedding would take place in a month's time and would Ivor and Vivienne please be there even for just a few days. Steven had arranged with Mariette's parents for them to possibly stay in the turret room upstairs.

"It has a fantastic view of Paris," he said. "And it's large and airy. A few stairs to climb but you are still agile, aren't you, Mom?"

Vivienne was delighted with the easy way Steven was talking. Obviously, things were going well for him and she knew in her heart that she was genuinely pleased for her son, even if her granddaughter would grow up in a country far away.

She said to Ivor, "You'll have to get a new suit, Ivor, one that is dressy enough for a Paris wedding."

"You mean I can't wear my beloved overcoat?" teased Ivor.

"No, of course you can't," said Vivienne firmly. "You are an artist, but this is one time you don't need to look like one."

Ivor laughed and hugged her. "Of course, I'll get myself to a tailor and let him kit me out," he said. "And I guess you'll be doing the same. Mother of the Groom and all of that."

"I hadn't thought of it," said Vivienne. "But yes, I'll look in these shops and I know I'll find the perfect outfit."

"Well, that's been a busy day," said Ivor. "What with Walter and painting and sorting his life and how Steven and Paris and sorting our lives. Time to sit and do nothing, dearest."

"That empty mind, Ivor," said Vivienne. "A glass of wine and some snacks might be nice…"

So they sat together, not talking, in companionable silence.

# Chapter 5

"I have to sort out details of this exhibition," Ivor said to Vivienne. "We are just an appetizer as it were, something interesting to kick off the day's talks and slide shows. An exhibition of large paintings will include my four- season ones. We will have a small room that will take just four working people for us to paint in. I will also paint and so will you, Vivienne, and we will have Walter and Curly as well. It doesn't matter what they paint and I am quite confident that Curly will come out tops. I still have to groom Walter. And this week, on Wednesday, we will meet locally and see what's up with him. We can group at the base of the mountain where that old shed is… there won't be any people there and I'd like him to be free of onlookers to paint. He might also like to talk …"

"And aren't you taking Curly?" asked Vivienne.

"No, not this time. Curly is fine and he can practice on his own. I need Walter to loosen up and to paint with confidence. He might also have more of his personal issues to talk about. It's not easy to paint your best when you are in the middle of marital problems."

So on Wednesday Ivor and Vivienne went to Ivor's studio. They waited there until Walter was dropped off by a taxi and approached the gate, which Ivor went to open. From the house, Vivienne could see Walter smiling as he greeted Ivor and she watched as the taxi drew off and the two men walked slowly along the path.

She knew not to wonder what they were talking about, but to stay in the moment, and just be herself. She smiled at Walter who greeted her cheerfully.

"So where are we going?" he asked.

Ivor answered that. "We will be walking up to the base of that mountain where there's an old wooden shed. And nice views either up the mountain or down across the tops of the town buildings to the ocean. You can choose what you want to paint, Walter."

"Yes, that will be good," said Walter. Then he added, looking at Vivienne, "I guess you want to know how I got on since last I saw you. I've been telling Ivor that we had some stormy days. But Cecile saw reason. I own the house so I am in it, in a separate bedroom, but that's ok. It's peaceful on my own.

"And Cecile is not accepting divorce, but I'm sure she sees that she and I have nothing at all in common."

"How did she like your painting of your feelings?" asked Vivienne.

"Ah. That really angered her. Wasting time, paper and paint with a mess like that. She went on quite a lot about my aimless life."

"I told her that was the mess I was in... I'm out of it to a degree. Just doing that painting helped a lot. I feel much better now that I have had my say, and am glad to be able to stay in the house even if she isn't cooking for me now..." He sighed. "But I can manage on toast and coffee for a few days."

Ivor was collecting the painting materials they would be needing for their morning's painting. He stopped to say to Walter, "You are nicely in control of your feelings now, anyway. You should be able to concentrate when you paint." He smiled at Walter.

"Well, I wouldn't have been able to paint last week," said Walter, "when we were at Julie's house. I was too distraught." He shook his head.

"Right, you are not there now," said Ivor. "You are here and we are just about ready to start on our walk up to the grassy part below the mountain. I have some cool drink for us as we may get thirsty …" and so the three of them set off.

Vivienne remembered the walk she'd taken with Ivor some time ago, but, today, she remembered it was a new day and she was a new person. A developing artist and now married to her tutor. She smiled. In a way, she was his tutor now, just supporting him and giving him the confidence he needed to grow both himself and his artists.

Walter was puffing a bit by the time they reached the grassy part with the trees and then there was the sudden sight of the old wooden shed. Vivienne saw Walter's eyes go from the shed up to the top of the white rocky mountains with the blue sky ahead. He turned and nodded to Ivor.

"Yes, I can paint here," he said. "It's quiet and natural. With no one about."

"Good," said Ivor. "I have watercolour paper for you that is on a board so it will stay firm when you paint. You'll find a water jar, paints, palette, and colours all in this bag. Find yourself a spot to sit in. I have a small folding stool also in this bag, so you can sit to paint. Find something to steady your water jar on. Remember. Get a still and silent mind first … empty your mind, then look at what you want to paint in a dreamy kind of a way. Absorb it into you. Do that for several minutes then close your eyes and see it in your imagination. Just stay in that silent relaxed frame of mind for a few minutes then, when you open your eyes, get your painting colours onto your palette. So what you then paint you have definite focus …" Then he added, "Remember, too, the dark contrasts. Don't be deliberate, but consciously be aware that contrasts bring a painting to life.

"Do not think while you are doing it. Just put blobs of paint around your palette. Then get your hake and soak it in water. You can then start painting. Paint with water first so that the paints run together when you paint. Have fun. I don't want an exact replica of what you are looking at and remember that white spaces are part of a painting.

"Above all, enjoy yourself and have fun." He met Walter's eyes and wordlessly they communicated, Vivienne saw it, and she knew Walter would be fine.

"Right, my lady," said Ivor to Vivienne. "You too are to paint with feeling and not aim for a photographic representation of what is here. Also, lots of white spaces are great in a painting. What you then paint has definite focus …" and then he added, "Remember, too, the dark contrasts. Don't be deliberate, but consciously be aware that contrasts bring a painting to life."

Vivienne remembered the last time she had been here. How far she had come in so many ways. She smiled at Ivor. "Thanks, Ivor."

She walked off with her bag of painting equipment to find a suitable place to paint a subject. She saw Ivor watching her and felt content. He was caring of her, she knew. She found a different aspect from the last time, a short bit of sandy road, and a gnarled tree bending over the road, a glimpse of the mountain behind, and set to work to leave out what she wasn't interested in and to paint, leaving lots of that rocky mountain. She had a very loose approach, with lots of white space, a bit of blue to represent the sky, and the mountain top soaring above the road and the tree. It was all done quickly as Ivor had taught her. *Stop before you think you are finished,* he had advised, so she did that.

An hour had gone by and there had been silence all the time. Again, it seemed that after an hour all three stopped at the same time and talking began.

Vivienne was looking at her painting. "I like it," she said proudly. "It's the best thing I've painted."

Ivor and Walter came over the look.

"Certainly, the eye is captivated by lots of white space, a small bit of blue sky, the rocky mountain and the twisty sandy road with the old bent tree pulling the eye towards it … it tells a story of its own," said Ivor musingly.

"Yes, true," said Walter. "Excellent, Vivienne, you are developing your own style. Lots of white space, not a lot of detail. Great."

"Now let's see what you have done, Walter," said Ivor.

"I took your advice, Ivor, and closed my eyes and let the scene impress itself on my subconscious. I felt that I needed peace and calm so my perspective was of the group of trees in darkish green at the side of a spring green grassy field with that old shed as a point of interest. I like what I painted. The shed is rather loosely painted, just indicating it rather than being precise."

"Walter, you have done exceedingly well," said Ivor, looking surprised. "If you carry on like this you will make me proud at our exhibition, which is a mere two weeks away."

Walter smiled. "I have set myself up a painting corner in my bedroom, undisturbed by Cecile. And I lock the door." He smiled. "It feels good to have some say over my life," he added.

Ivor chuckled. "Really Walter, you surprise me. So calm in such a storm."

"Thanks to the painting," said Walter. "I always knew it was what I needed."

"And what does Rose have to say?"

"Oh, she'd like to take up painting as well, so there is no trouble there," said Walter.

"All good stuff," said Ivor, who had painted a lovely scene of the distant ocean with the images of houses on the green grassy hillside.

"Time for refreshments," said Vivienne, unpacking cool drink and Ivor's famous almond cookies." She laughed. "He buys them by the hundred and freezes them. They taste fresh and so it was easy packing refreshments this morning."

The feeling of connectedness between them all brought their painting session to a satisfactory close. Refreshments over, the artists carefully carried their paintings and bag of materials back with them to Ivor's house, where Walter bid them goodbye and Vivienne and Ivor made for home.

Vivienne saw Ivor smiling into his beard and she rubbed his arm. "Happy, Ivor?" she asked.

"Oh yes, Vivienne. Walter far outstripped anything I expected and if he paints in his room as he says, he will be a star in a couple of weeks' time."

Vivienne had learnt to mind her own business, but she did take a moment to wonder how Cecile was dealing with an obviously unrepentant Walter.

At home, Ivor's cell phone rang. It was Walter.

"I don't know why I am phoning you," said a breathless Walter, "but I need an ear. Things here are chaotic. Cecile has been acting like a maniac. Whilst I was away, she went into my room and ripped up my painting of my feelings. She stamped on the pieces after throwing them at me, and has threatened to rip up everything I paint."

Ivor stood silently listening to Walter. Vivienne could clearly hear the conversation as Ivor had put it on speaker so Vivienne could listen.

At last, he said slowly, "Walter, that's bad news. After your good painting this morning."

"Yes, I know. I thought everything was under control, but it certainly isn't. Cecile doesn't want a divorce. Her lifestyle will change and she isn't prepared for that to happen."

Ivor looked at Vivienne.

"It's no good me offering advice to you, Walter," he said. "Try to keep everything on an even keel is all I can suggest. Not to rock the boat as it were."

"I'm afraid the boat is on very choppy waters, Ivor," said Walter. "It may be best if I move out, though it is my home."

"Maybe she will calm down by tomorrow," said Ivor.

"I don't think so," said Walter. "She is stamping around the house, slamming doors. I am in my room and the door is locked. I may just stay here without food," he said morosely.

"She will surely go to bed sometime," said Ivor. "Perhaps you can slip out and get a bite to eat then."

"That vampire is likely to stay up all night," said Walter. "She's not going to quieten down any time soon. I'll stay here and think what is best to do."

Ivor said, "Painting helped you. See if you can make some plan that includes painting. You need the practice and I need you..." he added wryly "... in one piece."

Walter snorted. "Throwing my painting at me didn't hurt, but she could use something more lethal. I never expected such a response from her."

"I'm sorry," said Ivor. "It was such a lovely morning."

"Agreed, Ivor, and this is my trouble, not yours. I thank you for listening. Even that has calmed me to a degree. I will just stay in my room. I'm unlikely to sleep."

"Yes, very wise," said Ivor. "But please ring me if you need anything at all, Walter. your wellbeing matters to me."

Vivienne looked at Ivor as he rang off.

"That was sound advice, Ivor," she said. "Walter will weather that storm. A bit of starvation is better than physical harm."

Ivor was looking troubled. Vivienne put her arm around him and gently hugged him. "Ivor, don't let it stress you. Somehow, your stress will add to Walter's burdens. Just send him love and light. And then let's have an early supper and decide how best we want to spend this evening."

Ivor had lightened up and he gave a small smile as he gently hugged Vivienne back.

"Beautifully said, dearest wife." He paused as he said that, looking slightly embarrassed. Then he added, "I never thought I'd ever have a wife."

"Well, you have one," said Vivienne with a smile, "and I have a nice curry and rice for tonight. How is that? Then I suggest we sit in the lounge and reminisce …"

"About what?" asked Ivor.

"Anything," said Vivienne. "Our childhood. Funny things that have happened. Let me get to know you more. We can each have a turn at talking. We need to know a lot more about each other than we do."

Ivor was reluctant, but agreed. "You start first," he said.

"Deal," said Vivienne.

Dinner over and the kitchen tidied up, Vivienne and Ivor repaired to the lounge.

"I'll start," said Vivienne. "I'll go back very far, to my childhood and the most vivid things that happened. I got chased by a bull and jumped into a haystack."

Ivor laughed. "How old were you, Vivienne?"

"About ten or eleven. I was staying on my uncle's farm and he had cattle that wandered around and he had a great big haystack, luckily surrounded by a sturdy split pole fence or the cattle would have eaten all the hay. I can't remember doing anything to particularly annoy the bull, but he came charging at me, head down and snorting. I grew wings and flew towards the hay stack and over the fence. I had to stay there for a long time as the bull didn't go away."

Ivor was thoughtful. "A bit like Walter with Cecile tonight," he said.

"Oh yes," said Vivienne. "Very apt. He will be safe it he can stick it out. Now your turn."

Ivor frowned. "You know I don't remember much of my childhood," he said.

"Well, anything," said Vivienne.

"All right, when I was living with the artist, Jed Huckleberry, I got chased by an aggro rooster that he had."

Vivienne laughed. "You're copying me," she said.

"No." said Ivor, "you just reminded me of that incident. That rooster had murderous intentions. I went into the fowl run to check for eggs. because Jed's wife wanted a couple of eggs. That rooster flew at me and pecked me so viciously I scrambled right out again.. And no, I didn't get the eggs his wife wanted."

Ivor was suddenly pensive. "This has opened some new insights for me," he said. "Jed helped me enormously. He got me to help him with his bit of home industry, which was healthy as it took my mind off myself. He got me to dig his garden and to plant seedlings. And water them …" Then he stopped. "Now I've told you a lot more than you've told me," he said.

"All right," said Vivienne. "I was an only child and my mother worked, so she wanted to find safe things for me to do in the holidays." She laughed. "But her brother, my uncle, wasn't the right person for that. He didn't have children and had no idea of how to look after me. There was a waterfall not far from house and he took me there one extremely hot day… and coming back up the gorge, I saw the tail of a snake sticking out from beneath a rock. I hit the rock and the snake turned round and spat in my face. A cobra. I ran like a mountain goat up the cliff until I reached a pool of water at the top of the falls where I washed my face and then there was the bull incident."

Ivor was silent. He put his arm around Vivienne. "This is great, Vivienne, recalling our young lives. I would like you to tell me more …" He hesitated. "I'm not trying to get out of talking about what I can remember. But getting to know you and how you became who you are is most enjoyable for me."

Vivienne turned and looked at him. She smiled and snuggled closer to him. "For me, it's so nice that I have someone to talk to, who is interested in what I have to say." Then she laughed. "There is so much to tell you, we will be occupied forever," she said. "But I would like to hear more bits of your life as we talk."

Their chat was interrupted by a phone call from Steven in Paris.

"Hi, Mom, I'm just checking on you and Ivor. The wedding will be small … I think the parents don't really want the world to know we had baby Violet before we got married, so there will be just about 40 people present. But it's still upper-class so Ivor can't wear his artist's jacket." He said this in a joking way and Vivienne took it as it was meant.

"We haven't forgotten, Steven, though I must admit we haven't thought of arrangements … getting to Paris, for instance, passports and so on, and I guess visas, and then our outfits. But we will start tomorrow, promise."

Steven sounded relieved. "Thank goodness you haven't completely forgotten, Mom," he said. "I do miss you and it will be wonderful to see you."

"Thanks, Steven, and how are Mariette and the baby Violet doing?"

"Oh, the baby is doing well. She was premature but is putting on weight nicely. And Mariette is a great mother," and he added proudly, "I'm a great dad too. I change nappies and feed Violet when Mariette is tired and wants to sleep."

"Of course, you are a great dad, Steven. You are always so caring of everyone and I imagine that little girl will love her kind daddy to bits." She was sincere as she said that and almost tearful. Steven had always thought of other people.

Ivor held her hand and squeezed it gently in a way to steady her and to remind her he was ready to bolster her in any way he could.

"Right, Steven," Vivienne finished the call by saying, "tomorrow, we will check on flights, passports and visas and I will give you details as soon as I have them myself."

She looked sober as she finished the call. "That is my tomorrow morning booked," she said to Ivor. "So I won't be coming with you when you finish your 'autumn' picture."

Ivor was still holding her hand. Now he released it but looked into Vivienne's eyes as he said, "Vivienne, you have no idea how your presence in my studio energizes me and, somehow, I get great ideas. I love my 'autumn' painting so far. All those lovely falling leaves in shades of gold and red, but the basis is there and I'll finish it on my own.. You have very important work to do."

This conversation put an end to their personal stories and shortly after Ivor was preparing for the next day and Vivienne was doing some cooking in the kitchen. As Ivor was passing by, she halted him. "I'll also check in some of the boutiques for fashionable outfits for both of us," she said.

"Horrors," said Ivor, with a small smile. "I hate to think what you will come up with … and what I will need to wear."

"Most certainly, dear heart," said Vivienne. "You will need a bit of a haircut, just a trim …"

They both laughed.

"You aren't going to interfere with my beard, I hope?" Ivor quipped.

"No, you look after that yourself very nicely," said Vivienne. "I'll just take care of the outer trimmings …"

They smiled at one another. Vivienne knew in that smile was the understanding she needed to search out the perfect outfits for them both. Tomorrow would be interesting.

# Chapter 6

The following day, after breakfast, Ivor set off by himself with his bag of art materials and wearing his precious loose jacket. Vivienne shook her head. She didn't think she'd ever seen Ivor without it and today's search for an outfit for the wedding was going to challenge her.

She began the day by phoning the airways about flights from Cape Town to Paris and found that would be easy. Passports would be in their hands in two weeks. Visas, a little bit of a challenge, and she decided she would leave dealing with them for another day when she had more time. They needed to go in personally and have their fingerprints and photos done digitally. She imagined that their next scheduled day out would be occupied in getting everything done so that everything was in order when the day arrived for them to fly.

A good deal of the morning had been taken up, but Vivienne wanted to do a quick search in a couple of the boutiques she had often passed by. She prepared lunch then she still had nearly two hours to explore fashions.

Down the front stairs of her townhouse she went, smiling at customers at the café, then going out into the street. She had often passed shops that proclaimed their stylish clothing was the perfect choice. She hurried up the street, glanced into one shop with clothes, but it didn't feel right to her. Another ten minutes and she saw a quaint corner shop that drew her attention.

She thought about what Ivor would look good in. He was tall and well- built. Big in fact. She couldn't imagine him in something colourful, Not black – it was too sombre for a wedding. Something classy. Understated. But stylish. She would ask the assistant when she was finished with customers in the back of the shop. She saw a striped suit and shuddered slightly. No pin stripes. No. Not black. No colours. *What would she find?*

The assistant had seen her and nodded, so Vivienne felt free to occupy herself in examining the mannequins kitted out in men's attire. She noted the pink and blue shirts, and the matching pink or blue hankie in the suit pocket. Ivor would shudder at such niceties, but would oblige. There were also shiny satin men's outfits in purple and blue. Vivienne shook her head. Not for Ivor.

She wasn't concerned for herself. She knew she would find something she liked.

But then in turning past a curtained area she came across mannequins, in pairs. A man and a woman mannequin in matching outfits. She smiled. What a revelation this would be for her son and his wife if they were to arrive dressed as a pair.

The mannequins were set apart from one another, pairs together. She looked at them. The satin outfit for both the man and woman she bypassed quickly. The pin-striped one caused her to pause as the woman had a lovely pin-striped jacket over a long grey dress. But it was too sombre.

This small shop had a long interior and Vivienne continued to explore. The mannequins were arranged as if they were walking together, spaced away from each other. Then she spied the perfect outfit for Ivor. Ivory white, with lapels of deep rose. It was rather startling, but the simplicity of the outfit entranced her.

The mannequin had a deep rose-pink handkerchief in its pocket and the shirt had deep-rose trimming down the front of a pale pinky-salmon colour shirt. There was also a matching tie in soft salmon pink with touch of deep rose at its end. This was eye-catching, but not bizarre … classy in a funny sort of way. And she liked it. She could see Ivor in it. And, what's more, the female mannequin in the pale pinky salmon coloured dress with matching jacket had a rose pink bodice and was stylish.

Vivienne knew the outfit on the male mannequin would be perfect for Ivor. He might jib a bit, but not much. It was classy and stylish and what was more, she loved the classic lines of the pale pinky salmon dress on the female mannequin. She touched the material and smiled. It felt wonderful. Cool, fairly heavy, but definitely uncrushable. Her eyes travelled from the top to the bottom of the dress with its bodice of deep rose-pink.

She looked at the matching jacket in the same pale pinky salmon material. From the elbows, the sleeves flared out and that material was the same deep rose as the bodice of the dress. Peering underneath the jacket, she saw that the dress had clean lines, with no other embellishments other than the deep-rose bodice. The dress had three-quarter sleeves, which gave it a

classy look and Vivienne liked it. *Would they have her size ...
36 medium?*

She held her breath. The blonde-middle-aged assistant was
coming her way and smiled at her. "You like this paired outfit,
I see," she said, eyeing Vivienne with a warm smile on her
face.

"Oh yes, very much," said Vivienne. "I was wondering if you
have it in my size ... thirty-six." She held her breath as she
asked, "and do you perhaps have the gent's outfit in a size 48?"

The assistant looked concerned. "I'll look," she said, "but the
gent's size is not one we normally stock."

"Please look," said Vivienne, now sure she had found the exact
outfits that might surprise her son and his wife, but wouldn't
disappoint.

"We usually order one of each size," the assistant said, "and
this has proved popular. You may be lucky, however."

She disappeared to the back of the shop. Vivienne was doing
her best to keep calm and to imagine the best, but it wasn't
easy. The assistant seemed to be taking a long time. She came
out holding just one box.

Vivienne's heart sank. *Which outfit wasn't available?*

The assistant said, looking apologetic. "Here is the size thirty-
six, which I am sure will fit you, but we have not got size forty-
eight in the man's outfit, I'm afraid."

"Oh dear." said Vivienne, quite distraught, despite the fact that,
just minutes ago, she hadn't even seen these paired outfits.

"Would you like to try on the dress, madam, while I make enquiries?"

Vivienne didn't even look at the price. It didn't matter what it cost. It was what she liked. She went into the curtained dressing room and took off her clothes. Slipping the long smooth material over her head felt wonderful and when the dress was properly on she looked at herself in the mirror. Her deep-blue eyes were sparkling. Her bobbed dark hair was a perfect contrast with the pale silky material with its deep rose bodice. The three-quarter sleeves looked good and when Vivienne added the jacket with the flared rose trimmed sleeves she smiled. It was the perfect outfit and a perfect fit. She undressed and put on her jeans and T shirt. Then she very carefully put the dress and jacket back on its hanger.

The assistant was outside looking troubled. She smiled when Vivienne was enthusiastic about the garment. "This is a dream of a dress," she said, "and it fits me perfectly."

"That is good news," said the assistant. "The not-so-good news is that a customer has taken the man's garments. She has added it to her account as she said she wanted it. However, there is a chance she may return it. She wasn't absolutely sure her husband would like it. He's more into the black and pin stripes," she said, "but hoped she could get him to be less conservative. I cannot tell you anything definite for now. Shall I put this dress aside for you, madam, just in case we can supply the gent's outfit?"

"Yes, please," said Vivienne, "and I'll pay a deposit if that is necessary."

"No," said the assistant. "If you can let me have your contact numbers and address that is all, thank you."

With that, Vivienne had to be content. She walked back quite slowly to her house. She was wondering what Ivor would say about it if they found the size she thought would fit. And when he returned from a clearly successful day at completing the 'autumn' painting, he found a sombre Vivienne.

Ivor came into the kitchen with a light in his eyes and small smile. Vivienne knew that day had been good for him.

"Why so gloomy, dearest one?" he asked gently, the smile leaving his face as he took off his loose overcoat and hung it behind the kitchen door.

Vivienne gave him his now customary hug, staying in his arms a little longer than usual.

"Well, what is it Vivienne?" he asked.

"I've been out looking for outfits for us for Steven's wedding," she said.

Ivor hugged her. "Oh, that is such a serious business now, isn't it?"

He was teasing her to get her to lighten up.

"Ivor, it's serious. It really is," she said.

"Tell me about it," he said, taking a seat on the kitchen chair. "I'm listening."

"Ivor, it's hard to explain but I found the perfect outfit for you and for me. Matching outfits, as it were."

"Oh really," said Ivor. "Now I'm getting suspicious and maybe understand your gloom, but continue."

"I'd prefer if you could see the dress, with a matching jacket, on me rather than me tell you about it," Vivienne said earnestly, "but the problem is they don't have that particular matching outfit in your size."

"Well, that's good," said Ivor. "Maybe I don't need an outfit."

"Of course, you do," said Vivienne forcefully.

"Though I guess you might feel uncomfortable without that inseparable part of you ..." She laughed and tousled Ivor's hair. "And you will need a visit to a hairdresser," she said solemnly.

"Alright, so my life is changing," said Ivor smiling. "I'm a bit in awe of what outfit you are hoping to kit me out in."

"First, we have to pray that woman who has it out on appro doesn't like it and returns it to the shop. Hold your breath for that to happen."

And happen it did.

The next morning, Vivienne got a phone call from the boutique. "You're in luck, Mrs Murphy," the assistant said. "That size forty-eight suit has been returned ... now we just have to hope your husband approves and that it fits him."

"How exciting!" said Vivienne. "We will be in as soon as possible."

It was a Saturday and Ivor was having a lazy start to the day but all this changed as an excited Vivienne startled him as he lay in bed.

"Ivor, please get up and get dressed. The boutique has phoned and the gent's suit is back ... the man didn't like it...." She hesitated and looked at him directly. "I hope *you* like it ..."

"Won't you tell me a bit about it," teased Ivor, sitting up in bed. "Just so that I am prepared."

"Not at all," said Vivienne firmly. "That will spoil the surprise for you..." She smiled, leant over and ruffled Ivor's hair, adding, "Yes, a visit to the hairdresser is essential."

"Oh, having a wife does mess with life," said Ivor in jest, but getting out of bed at the same time and adding. "Give me fifteen minutes and I'll be dressed and ready..."

In fifteen minutes time, Ivor, wearing a blue checked shirt, now sporting no missing buttons, put on his beloved overcoat and declared that he was ready.

"Lead on, Macduff," he said.

Vivienne smiled. Ivor was taking this all in his stride. She just hoped he wasn't too shocked at her choice of outfit for him. They went together out of the front door. Down the stairs and past the café below. The smells of meat frying and of chips and other delicacies, no doubt caused Ivor to say to Vivienne, "After the visit to the boutique, can we go to the café with my paintings and have a full English cooked breakfast? I know you make great breakfasts, but let's do something different. I also would like to see if my recent paintings are selling or not."

So, arm in arm they walked up the street to the quaint boutique on the corner of a lane.

"Here," said Vivienne, "in here."

Ivor stopped and looked in the window. Vivienne winced. The coupled mannequins were displaying a deep-blue satin man's suit with a matching woman's outfit also in satin.

Ivor turned to look at Vivienne and said solemnly in an undertone, "I'm not even going in if you are kitting me out in satin."

Vivienne laughed. "You can't be such a coward, Ivor, Surely you want to see what I've chosen?"

"I'm nervous," said Ivor. "Very nervous."

"All the same, come on, let's go in," said Vivienne, leading him in by the hand.

The shop assistant who had served her recognized her instantly and smiled.

"Nice to see you," she said, and looking at Ivor, she added, "I see why you wanted a size 48. Would you like to follow me, sir? Come and see your wife's choice for you."

Vivienne smiled to herself. She could sense Ivor's nervousness and in such a big man, it was almost funny. But at the same time, it wasn't funny. What if Ivor objected?

They passed several rows of dress racks then went past the curtained area to the show room where the mannequin couples were arranged so they were walking down the aisle. Ivor shuddered at the sight if the pin- striped man's outfit.

"So sombre," he said, "I hope that isn't your choice, my adventurous wife."

"No," said Vivienne, "but you have to understand we need to look outstanding for that Paris wedding."

"Humph," said Ivor, still walking slowly along and looking at the coupled mannequins. Then round a corner they came across the outfits Vivienne had chosen. The male mannequin had its back facing Ivor so his eyes just caught sight of the off-white, creamy colour of the jacket and trousers.

"Now that looks like something I might wear," he said.

Vivienne held her breath. What would he say to the two narrow lapels in deep-rose… the pale pinky salmon shirt and the deep rose hankie in the pocket of the jacket?

She was not disappointed. On walking around the model, Ivor shook his head. "I could never…" he said.

"Never what?" asked Vivienne.

"Never wear an outfit like that."

"Oh, Ivor, you haven't properly looked at it."

"I've seen enough to know I wouldn't wear it."

"Look at my outfit," said Vivienne, hoping to switch his focus.

He looked at the model in the elegant heavy silk gown in a very soft shade of pinky salmon. It had a bodice of a deep-rose colour, and the slim skirt was classy with its smooth lines that ran from below the bodice. The jacket with three-quarter sleeves that flared out where the deep-rose was joined to the pale, pinky-salmon material was elegant and outstanding. Ivor studied it carefully then looked at Vivienne.

"You will look wonderful in that outfit," he said. "I heartily approve. It is perfect for you."

"But I need my partner in his outfit, too, Ivor," she pleaded. "Won't you at least try it on and I'll try on the woman's outfit then we can look at ourselves in that large mirror. Please say you will."

Ivor looked at Vivienne. She could see in his eyes his wish to please her, but he had his own doubts about the gent's outfit.

He shook his head.

Vivienne tried again.

"Ivor if you really hate it, I won't take my outfit either and we'll look elsewhere for outfits for us both, but please won't you just give these a chance?"

Ivor at first shook his head. Vivienne looked at him and the pleading look on her face made him laugh.

"You are a very manipulative wife," he scolded her gently. "I'm promising nothing, but I will try it on, just to please you." Then he added hopefully, "Maybe it won't fit me."

"You are to put on the shirt, tie and jacket with the hankie, the whole outfit," said Vivienne.

"Goodness, I'll be all day getting dressed," said Ivor. "… Never in my life have I had to endure such …"

"Such what?" said Vivienne.

"Such *indignities,*" said Ivor. "I'm a respectable artist, and this looks like some fancy dress costume."

"You *are* a respectable artist," agreed Vivienne, "and a respectable artist who is going to a very respectable wedding in Paris. If he and his wife look a bit different, people will always remember them and they are coming from a foreign country. Aren't they … from Africa …?"

"Oh, let's stop talking and get the fitting done," said Ivor, nodding to the assistant who de-robed both mannequins and handed each set of garments to Vivienne and Ivor.

"The dressing room for gents is in that corner," said the assistant, and to Vivienne, "You remember where the ladies change rooms are, don't you?"

Vivienne nodded then said to Ivor, "See you in ten minutes' time. And we'll walk together towards that large mirror over there and see what we look like. Please reserve judgment until the walk takes place. Okay, Ivor?"

"Deal," said Ivor, smiling at Vivienne and adding. "You are really persistent, but I guess I like it." With a relaxed gait, he went towards the gents' change room.

Vivienne was excited. In the ladies' change room, she discarded her clothes and, almost lovingly, slipped the smooth heavy silky dress over her head and zipped it up. The bodice sat comfortably above the classic lines of the dress, giving her a most elegant look. She smoothed the three-quarter sleeves approvingly and slipped on the jacket. It felt lovely and the flared parts from below the elbows fascinated her. It teamed beautifully with the deep rose of the bodice and Vivienne felt it was the loveliest outfit she'd ever tried on.

She smoothed her hair, and then with a smile went out of the change room to wait for Ivor. She was facing the long wide mirror and, even at a distance, she loved what she saw.

She thought of Lady Lavender talking of thoughts like wild horses and gently bringing them back into the stable. So, by the time Ivor came out of the gents' change room, she was calm. It was just as well as she was ready to laugh at Ivor. It wasn't the outfit, it was that he looked so totally different. Different from the usual large man with a checked shirt and loose overcoat. Now coming towards her was a completely different man.

His bearded face and shoulder-length hair didn't detract from the elegant gentleman in an ivory-white outfit with slim rose lapels and a rose hankie in the pocket. The pale pinky salmon shirt was the exact match with her dress and on the whole, the look was flawless.

"Come and we will walk together towards that mirror," she said, and they turned to face the large mirror in the distance.

"Come walk with me," said Vivienne. She saw the assistant watch in amusement as Ivor had a recalcitrant attitude to walking with Vivienne, clearly feeling foolish, but she stood waiting for him. He sighed, let her take his arm and turned to face the mirror in the distance.

Then he said, "I simply don't recognize that chap in that fancy suit," and he looked at Vivienne. "Do you know who he is?"

As they walked slowly towards the mirror, the smiling assistant was clapping. "You make a stunning couple," she said. "I'm so glad that customer returned the gent's outfit …don't you think so?"

Vivienne definitely thought so, but she wanted Ivor to approve before she voiced her strong opinion. She said gently, "But Ivor, don't you think that man looks classy?"

"I'm an artist and classy isn't something we talk about," he said.

"Well, let's forget you are an artist and think of you as an ordinary man getting a new outfit."

"But I'm not an ordinary man," objected Ivor.

"For this wedding you might just have to change your identity…," said Vivienne.

"Sir, you look wonderful," said the assistant. "The suit on you looks far better than it did on the hanger. It was made for you and I'm not just saying that. I genuinely think it is perfect for you."

Ivor was hesitating. Vivienne didn't say anything. She wanted him to make up his own mind.

"I suppose you might select some dreadful purple satin suit if I don't take this," he said semi-jokingly.

"Oh yes," said Vivienne "there's purple and deep-blue in lovely satin if you'd prefer ..." They both laughed.

Ivor turned to the assistant. "Thank you for your comments. They helped me to decide. It will be for only one afternoon, so I will be a cooperative husband and thank my dear wife ... and you ... for choosing this outfit for me."

Vivienne would have hugged Ivor but thought better of it. Better to keep the outfits looking new rather than for her to crumple any part of it.

"Thank you, now let me go and disrobe," said Ivor, "and we will see you at the counter." Then he smiled at Vivienne. "Are you happy, my dear wife? I must say you look splendid in that outfit and your son will be thrilled with you. And that's important to you, Vivienne, isn't it?"

Strangely, it wasn't so important anymore. Her life with Ivor was the important thing and being part of it was even better.

She nodded her acquiescence and she, too, headed for the change room to take off her new outfit.

Back at the counter, Ivor produced a bank card to pay for the outfits. He didn't query the price, which was expensive, and neither did Vivienne. What mattered was that they both were happy. On their way out, she did notice Ivor giving a disapproving look at the male mannequins in satin suits. She giggled to herself and held Ivor's arm firmly.

"I'm not going to run away," Ivor said to her.

"Maybe not, but I'm just so happy, Ivor, that we have found matching outfits that we both like. And you do like it, don't you, Ivor."

"I'm not sure about that," said Ivor. "I didn't recognize the man in that suit and that troubled me."

"Oh, Ivor, what does it matter what you wear? Underneath, you are the same person you've always been, and I know it and you know it."

In the street, she gave him a hug.

That day, as they were putting away their new outfits, the phone rang.

It was Walter – a Walter back in a state of despair. Ivor put his cell phone on speaker so Vivienne could hear, too.

"Ivor, things are not going well here," the distraught man said. "I went out to see Rose as I needed her refreshing presence. I never realized how dour and boring Cecile is. She is only concerned with material things, what she looks like and what others think of her. Her car and where she shops and all sorts are to me irrelevant things. I told you I took the art class to give me something to fill my mind with that interested me… but she has said all along it's a waste of time and money and that I should be mowing the lawn or digging earth to make a front garden. We can always get a gardener to do that. I can afford it, but she wants me occupied in the way she thinks I should be.

"I'm sorry to go on, but while I was out visiting Rose she went into my room and destroyed all the paintings I've been doing. And she squirted out my paints so I have nothing to paint with. I can't tell you how much it upset me."

Ivor looked at Vivienne. She was quiet, just watching Ivor.

Then Ivor said, "The big thing is to get control of your emotions Walter. You can always buy new paints and paper. The intrusion into your private life is what you need to deal with."

"Like I told you, she won't give me a divorce, Ivor. She wants to keep up her life style."

"Then why don't you let her have it, Walter, and just move out?" asked Ivor. "And don't go back. I suggest you remain generous and keep the lights on and whatever other running expenses you have, and find some quiet corner for you to live in? Perhaps near to your work? I wouldn't suggest being near to Rose as I feel you need to stabilize yourself first. Get on an even keel and respect yourself. Do that and probably the thing with Rose will turn out okay."

Walter was listening. He sighed. "That does make sense, Ivor," he said. "And I have my own car, so it wouldn't disrupt Cecile at all. Just talking to you makes me feel better. I've always been too pliant with Cecile. Done whatever she has asked. It's always been easier that way, but I have not been happy. I'll think it out on my own now, thanks, Ivor."

Ivor said in an encouraging voice, "Keep up your spirits and please keep in touch. Remember I need you as a creative artist in two weeks' time. We can practice again next week if you like."

Walter seemed to be thinking as he was quiet.

"I guess I can make sense of my life," he said, "and I can calm down. Just being away from Cecile will help."

He thanked Ivor and rang off.

Vivienne said, "You helped Walter, Ivor."

"He needs to help himself," said Ivor. "Been a doormat all his married life, it seems." And he fondly put his arm round Vivienne. "You wouldn't use me as a doormat, would you? But I guess I'll have to watch you," he was teasing now, "with the kind of clothing you are kitting me out in."

On this lighter note, they got on with their day with Ivor saying, "I just have the big painting of 'winter' to do and my commission is done. So will you be able to come with me tomorrow morning, Vivienne? It does help just having you there."

Vivienne smiled at him. "Yes, Ivor, I'll take pen and paper and work out what we need to do to organize ourselves properly for Paris. We will need to buy a present for the new baby and wedding present for the bride and groom and a present for the parents. .. for having us to stay."

"Goodness all that planning," said Ivor.

"Plus the bookings," said Vivienne.

"And remember to plan for my exhibition, just over a week away now," said Ivor thoughtfully. "I do hope Walter sorts himself out. He needs his own space and he'll have to buy new tubes of paint and paper. Lucky we use just a limited palette."

"But it has been a constructive day," said Vivienne. "We have our outfits and Walter got some good advice from you." Then she added, "We both need to buy new shoes for the wedding and I might need a headdress of some sort and a bag and gloves, so we'll be going back to the boutique some time."

"Humph, that spoils my night," said Ivor, clearly thinking of those outfits.

"You looked superb, Ivor," said Vivienne firmly. "So, we need to complete the picture with shoes and for me, a matching handbag and headdress. We can go one afternoon after you've finished your day's work, Ivor, I'd like to get everything sorted and, in the meantime, there are lovely gift shops just up the streets. One afternoon, I'll check for those presents we need."

Ivor yawned. "All this has exhausted me. Do you mind if I take a rest now, Vivienne?

"Of course not, said Vivienne. "You go and rest and I'll sort out dinner." She smiled to herself as she watched Ivor amble off to the bedroom. Who would have thought it would be so much better here? *With Ivor in her life it certainly was*

# Chapter 7

Very early the next morning, the phone rang. It was Walter.

"Ivor, do you mind if I join you in your studio today and do some painting? I need to get back into the mood ... I have bought new paints and paper and I may also bounce some ideas off you, if you don't mind."

Ivor looked at Vivienne and she nodded. "Fine, Walter, we'll see you there say at nine o'clock."

Ivor and Vivienne were in Ivor's studio and Ivor had organized himself and a space for Walter. Vivienne knew not to ask him if Walter would disturb him, because she knew his method was to let Walter talk and then to occupy Walter with painting. He became so absorbed he didn't talk at all and also in that silence, ideas began taking place for Ivor.

Walter arrived in a taxi at exactly nine o'clock. "My own car is in my garage at home. It would cause drama for me to go and fetch it. So, it's best this way. I simply bought some new clothes and shaving outfit and found a bed and breakfast not far from my work, so I have had peace." He was talking straight away and obviously had a lot he wanted to get off his chest.

Ivor let him in to the house and led him to the studio. "Or would you like to sit on the porch with a cup of coffee first and tell me what has transpired?" asked Ivor.

"Yes, thanks, that's a great idea," said Walter gratefully.

Vivienne nodded. "Coffee coming up in a jiffy," she said.

So Ivor and Walter repaired to the porch and sat down, while Vivienne went and busied herself in the kitchen making coffee. She was soon back with the coffee and the usual almond cakes, to where the two men sat on the porch, with the colourful indoor plants giving a cheerful feel to the place.

Walter sighed. "You feel like family to me," he said.

"We are family," said Ivor. "You are very important to me as a developing artist, Walter. So let's hear the latest update."

"I've switched my cell off so I couldn't take calls from Cecile," he said. "She will bug me if she can. So it's best if she doesn't know where I am. I did leave her a message, so she won't send the police looking for me, telling her I was moving out.

"And though I didn't sleep, it was just a good time to look back at my life. I realize that our marriage has been all about Cecile and what she wants. The pity is that she never laughs or jokes, and she criticizes everything I do. I don't know why. She is punishing me in some way for deficiencies I have. I have just given in to her. Taking your art course was my first step in making something happen for me and, of course, meeting Rose made me start thinking of what I am losing out on in life. Just the simple appreciation of daily life. It isn't there. So my start is to move out. I will build up slowly. But my needs are few. I have a small hardware shop and have to run that. The bed and breakfast will serve me very well."

He paused for breath. Ivor had been listening carefully and nodded his head. His hazel eyes were serious. "Take care in thinking this out, Walter. I go along with the Buddhist philosophy … be generous in all endings. So if this is an ending, do not hurt Cecile. She is going to be hurt enough with you out of her life even if you do allow her to stay in the house and pay the bills."

"Yes, all of that," said Walter. "My business can afford all of that."

Then he smiled. "And I will be able to see Rose more often. She may even start working for me."

"Well, that's a good idea," said Ivor.

"Yes, she needs a job and I need an assistant. So I can see her that way and we can see if our relationship is serious or not."

Walter had finished his coffee and stood up.

"Ivor, I'm ready to paint," he said. "I want to put my all into painting this morning. To get back the great joy I got from your course."

"Excellent," said Ivor, standing up. "Let's take our cups and plate to the kitchen, and then it's off to the studio. And, thanks, Vivienne. Will you be watching the weaver build another nest?"

"Oh no," said Vivienne. "I have to make lists now … of things we have to shop for," she smiled at Ivor, "like shoes from that lovely boutique."

He smiled back at her and softly ruffled her hair. "You know what to say to inhibit the painting gene," he said.

"Oh, nothing will stop that, Ivor, I know your passion for painting." She smiled at the two men, who sent off to the studio to start their morning of painting.

Vivienne spent a short time in the kitchen tidying up then she joined Ivor and Walter in the studio. Her chair faced the garden and the tree with now a couple of weavers' nests, hanging on it. She had a pen and some paper and was ready to spend a quiet few hours going over all there was to do with arrangements, both for Paris and for the painting exhibition. She knew that Ivor would deal with the painting side of it, but there were still arrangements to make that perhaps he had forgotten about. There was Curly to consult with and Walter. She needed to find out where they were to do their exhibition and what they needed to bring to make it professional and easy for the artists. She would like to look at the venue. Where it was, how big, if they had tables for the artists and easels. When to start, and were the visitors allowed to come into the venue and watch? She felt nervous at this as she would also be on exhibition.

In between her serious thoughts, she heard Walter talking to Ivor.

"I'm so grateful for the chance to do watercolour painting," he was saying. "Cecile, of course, thinks I should be doing manual labour, and that spoils it for me. I would love to be left alone for some hours to paint. I've always been interested in painting, but never imagined I could paint myself."

"Well," said Ivor, "you need to get going with practicing and you have found a bed and breakfast that will take care of your meals. Do they supply dinner as well?"

"They do."

"That's good. What time you have over from working, you need to apply yourself seriously to painting. We learnt lots of techniques on our course... and you need to practice each of them. You will be on display in just over a week's time and people can come in and watch you paint."

"That's scary," said Walter,

"Not if you've practiced," said Ivor. "Now it's time for you to start. I think start with a sky. Cloudy with a bit of darkness in one corner. Use two-thirds of your paper then later do a foreground. It you have a rich sky, you will need a simple foreground. Alright?"

"Yes," said Walter, "I've got it and will do it."

"Thanks," said Ivor, "as I have to paint my 'winter' scene. I usually talk it over with Vivienne, but didn't today. So, I'll just have to use her energy and dream it up myself, which I know I can do....so let's get to it, Walter."

Vivienne watched as both men involved themselves with their palettes and squirted out blobs of different paints from different tubes. Soon, each man was in a world of his own.

Vivienne stood up as Ivor dropped water onto some of the blobs of paint and, seemingly, was in a no-work mode. But she knew that mode. It was the idling that went before the creative spark emerged. She smiled as she thought how much she enjoyed puddling with paint. After a few minutes of doing nothing much, Ivor's large hake brush suddenly developed energy that seemed to belong to it alone. Ivor was holding it, but long paint strokes of pure water followed by swirls of pale-blue, made for a pale winter sky with a sun not properly awake. Ivor was dropping in pale-blue paint for distant mountains with a foreground of vibrant sunshine-yellow and a path in slightly deeper sand colour.

Vivienne was still standing watching Ivor who used the hair dryer to dry the background. Now came winter trees, grand old trees with peeling dark bark resting during the winter months, their leaves lying in piles on the ground. A small muddy river, with some bulrushes with long red ends to them gave some unexpected colour and drew one's eye to that corner of the painting ... then led to the sandy path, ending in the sandy section in the middle. It was a winter scene, trees resting without their leaves. There was much still to do, but Ivor had done the basis and the rest would be completed the following day.

Vivienne turned around and found a chair to sit in. She was aghast that she had been watching Ivor paint and had not done the lists which she had intended to do. She wondered how Walter was faring. He, too, had a busy sky, from what she could see, with storm clouds building up on one side. Vivienne nodded her head. Yes, Walter had used counterchange and had a dark shed in the opposite corner at the bottom of the painting. So one's eyes followed through from the shed, along the green landscape and then to distant hills, with faint blue mountains behind then the threatening sky above.

It was very pleasing to the eye. She saw Walter put down his brush, wash and wipe it and then glance around, looking pleased.

Ivor was also completing what he was doing, so Walter said hesitantly, "It is okay if I talk, Ivor?"

"Yes, go ahead," said Ivor.

"You cannot know what this painting does for me, Ivor. I was totally absorbed in what I was doing and enjoyed it, I was in the scene as it were and now, that I've finished it, I look at it and can enjoy that serene countryside. It makes me feel serene, too. And how can that be when I have this chaos in my life?"

Vivienne interrupted Walter. "Don't think... I have learnt that from both Ivor and a teacher friend. It's the thinking that's the problem."

"That's all very well," said Walter, "but I keep on going back to the scene with Cecile, my paints all squashed out, my paintings torn up ..."

Ivor nodded at Vivienne and added, "Walter, don't bring the past into the present. And like Vivienne is telling you, stay in the moment. Keep watching yourself, and just stay in the now. No thought of yesterday or tomorrow. Of course, you have to make plans, but, once you've done that, carry them out and watch yourself – stay in the present moment. I know you are pulling through. The painting you have done today is a winner."

"Thank you," said Walter. "I feel like a new man."

"Keep feeling that way," said Ivor, "and learn to make time for yourself to paint and during the time you paint, just be at one with the paints and the paper. It will help you. Your wife will need to deal with her own problems herself. You are not there to be chastised or bullied, Walter. Remember that."

Walter straightened up. Vivienne was glad to see that. When he went to Julie's, his shoulders were hunched as if the world was sitting on them. Today, he looked like a new man.

"And Rose? What happened there?" asked Ivor.

"Oh, Rose is adaptable and also empathetic. She has kept out of my way as I have not been ready to talk to her, but she understands my need to be alone, and also to get into this painting," He looked at Ivor, "not only for your exhibition but because it is good for my soul..." He smiled and added, "It really is."

"Well, we have had a good day, Walter," said Ivor. "I leave it to you to contact me should you feel the need, but I think you will be able to weather this storm on your own. Remain quiet yourself, Walter. And keep your mind from thinking."

Vivienne smiled at Walter. "That's true, Walter, but hard, I know, as I've been there, but just watch your thinking ... and pull it back to the present moment."

Ivor and Walter were cleaning up after their painting session when Vivienne stood up. "Anyone like tea, or coffee, or a cool drink?"

"Yes, please, coffee for me," said Ivor.

"I'll have a cool drink, please, Vivienne," said Walter.

"And I'll join you in a coffee," said Vivienne.

"We'll have our drinks out on the porch," said Ivor, "then we will all be on our way. And, thank you, Walter, for your cooperation today. The exhibition is important for me as I am building a reputation, not only as an artist but as an art teacher. I must say, I do enjoy the teaching. It is great to see the development of all. Vivienne here is doing famously. We are due to go on another day's painting."

"Oh no," said Vivienne, "that day's painting has to give over to planning … not only your exhibition, but remember we have a wedding in Paris and presents to buy, not to mention…," she smiled, "… shoes to buy and a hairdresser to visit."

Walter looked intrigued.

"It's my son's wedding in Paris," said Vivienne, "and he invited us to be present."

Walter looked at Ivor and smiled. "Wearing that artist's smock, Ivor?" he asked.

They all laughed and Vivienne was glad to see that he was able to identify with them and also to see a bit of humour in it all. She smiled to herself. The humour of the satin men's outfits was a quick flash in her mind and brought a broader smile.

"Well, on that note I see my taxi is here," said Walter. "So thank you both for a very uplifting morning." He nodded, and again Vivienne was glad to see he had an easy walk with head up high as he made his way to the gate.

The following morning, Ivor put finishing touches to his "winter" painting, declared he was satisfied with it and he and Vivienne returned home early. .

"Let's have an early lunch and then visit that boutique and look for shoes ... ones that suit our matching outfits and each other."

"Do we really have to go there," asked Ivor.

"Most certainly, Ivor," said Vivienne. "Let's eat quickly and then off we go."

An hour later, Ivor and Vivienne had locked up and were walking up the street passing many interesting shops, which Vivienne now knew she wanted to explore more thoroughly. She had three very important presents to buy, but the shoes were the present priority.

As they reached the boutique and entered it, Vivienne noticed Ivor looking doubtful.

"Ivor, don't have second thoughts. You are an artist and I love my outfit. Please let's just see if they have shoes to match. We know the colour. Off-white for you, and I'm not sure about me..." she hesitated and looked at Ivor. "I was wondering about rose shoes with a very small heel... it would tie in with the trims on my dress and jacket."

Ivor shook his head. "You decide, dearest one," he said. "This is out of my league."

"All right, thanks Ivor," said Vivienne. "I'll ask them and see what they have in stock. Isn't this exciting?"

"I don't know that I agree with you," said Ivor. "I actually find it frightening. What's wrong with my usual shoes?" He put forward a large foot wearing soft leather sandals that showed his toes.

Vivienne laughed. "Really, Ivor how can you suggest such a thing? And, of course, you will need socks. Something you don't wear."

"Socks?"

"Yes, socks that go on your foot before the shoes … we will ask what they have."

"Oh, preserve me," said Ivor, "for all I know you'll be asking for rose- coloured socks for me."

"Now that is an idea," said Vivienne with a smile, "but maybe off- white with a rose trim… how would that be, Ivor, maybe, rose motif up the sides…?"

"What have I got myself into?" groaned Ivor. "I don't think I've ever been into a shop like this." But Vivienne could see a small sparkle in his eyes and the slightest smile. He's enjoying this, she thought.

"But, yes, Ivor, let's ask for rose socks or a pale-pink to match your shirt." She said this in the most guileless tone.

"You're teasing me, Vivienne," said Ivor.

"Not at all, Ivor," said Vivienne. "You need shoes and you need socks to match your outfit. Perhaps," and she smiled at him, "we can ask them to bring a selection of suitable socks, large size, off white, off-white with rose motif, rose colour and pale-salmon colour."

They hadn't noticed the assistant standing just behind them.

"Yes, madam, I remember what you bought the other day and we will certainly bring out those socks you mentioned. If you'll give me few minutes."

"And also shoes. Where do we look for them?"

"The shoes are over on that side," said the assistant, pointing to the opposite side of the boutique.

"Thanks," said Vivienne, "Let's start with the socks and if you have them, stockings for me, or half-stockings also in the pale-salmon colour, though I guess I should look for shoes first…"

"The stockings are sheer, so I don't think the shoes you choose will affect the choice of stocking," said the assistant. "Let me look."

She was off, leaving Ivor and Vivienne alone.

Ivor looked at Vivienne with a smile. "Lucky, we have only one child getting married," he said. "And I guess this is just the start of it."

"Let's enjoy the ride, Ivor," said Vivienne. "It's something different for both of us and I'm looking forward to wearing that dress."

She turned and gave Ivor a lovely smile. "You'll have to think of places to take me where I can wear that dress afterwards. It can't just hang it in my cupboard."

"Yes, agreed," said Ivor, with a smile, "but don't think I'm wearing that rather outrageous outfit of mine again."

"Oh, Ivor," said Vivienne in mock distress. "You won't know yourself in it."

"That's what worries me," said Ivor, still smiling. "I won't know myself."

"But, surely you'll wear the trousers?"

"Well, maybe, though I'm not a trouser man."

They stopped their light-hearted banter as the assistant came back with an armful of boxes.

She set them down carefully.

"Let's start with the stockings." She opened the top box. "Knee- length is all you need," she said. "In a sheer light flesh colour."

"Perfect," said Vivienne. "Thank you."

She eyed the assistant with a smile. "But what we really want to see are the men's socks for my husband to select his."

The assistant opened the top box. "A pair of plain off-white men's socks."

"Very nice," said Ivor, "Can we settle for those?"

"Let's rather see what is in the other boxes," said Vivienne, looking at Ivor with a smile. "There might be a better choice,"

"I knew you'd say that," sad Ivor, with a smile. "All right let's see what you have."

The first box shook both Ivor and Vivienne. Looking at them was a pair of deep rose-pink socks, men's size.

"Oh no," said Ivor. "Never. Not those."

Vivienne laughed. "Ivor, they would be perfect."

"Let's see in the other boxes," said Ivor hastily.

The next box held a pair of plain salmony pink socks. Ivor considered them.

"They are the exact colour of your shirt," the assistant said, "and would look very elegant."

Ivor sniffed.

"Now let's see what is in the last box," said the assistant.

This box held an off-white pair of socks with a rose-coloured motif of a slender diamond pattern running up the outside of each sock.

"How do you like these," asked the assistant. "The rose-coloured diamond pattern is not likely to be very visible as the trousers will reach down to your shoes, but that touch of rose matches the touch of rose down the centre of the shirt ..."

Surprisingly, Ivor said, "I rather like them, Vivienne. What do you think?"

Vivienne was surprised. She thought Ivor would choose the off-white socks or flesh-colour socks ... but he was an artist.

Ivor smiled at the assistant. "I am getting into the feeling of being someone different, even for just one afternoon. So, yes, I'd like these socks, please." He smiled at Vivienne. "I might even like wearing them when the wedding is over."

"Oh Ivor, really?" said Vivienne. "Then you'll have to start wearing shoes."

"Which takes us over the shoes now, thank you very much," said Ivor, as the assistant walked with them carrying two boxes they would be buying and three to put back on the shelves.

At the shoe section, the men's shoes were on one side and the women's on the other.

"You go and look for off-white shoes, Ivor, and perhaps try the socks on with them," said Vivienne. "To see they are not too big or too small. I'll browse amongst the woman's shoes. If that's okay?"

"Certainly," said Ivor walking over the Men's section whilst Vivienne looked at the array of shoes. All sizes, all shapes, all colours, with heels and without heels.

She decided on a fairly flat shoe and that led her to a section with gold shoes, silver shoes, and rose-coloured shoes. But no off-white shoes. There were white shoes but she didn't think they would look nice with her pale-salmony pink dress. She tried to picture her feet and the dress. She didn't like to admit it, but she rather liked the deep-rose shoes with just the slightest heel. She squinted her eyes looking at the shoes and imagining the pale-salmony pink dress with the flared three-quarter rose-coloured sleeves and the rose bodice. And she just knew the rose shoes were what would be perfect.

She looked for her size. The assistant found a pair size 6 and Vivienne tried them on. They were soft and lovely to wear. She knew the shoes were meant for her.

She smiled at the assistant as she took them off.

"I can just see them balancing perfectly the rose bodice and rose sleeves of the jacket … They are perfect, thank you so much."

The assistant smiled at her. "There is another thing you need, Madam," she said, "It's called a fascination and it's to put on your head … it's just a small bit of net with a flower, a deep-rose-coloured flower in your case. That too will match the shoes."

"Oh, wonderful," said Vivienne. "May I come with you to look?"

The shoes were packed in a box and Vivienne held them as they went to the counter with the headdresses. What an array there were. Nets of different colours. And decorations of different types, even feathers, but the assistant found what

Vivienne needed. A deep rose-pink rose with a small bit of pale-salmon-pink veiling.

"That will go perfectly with your dress, madam," said the assistant earnestly. "I am sure you will have a wonderful day at the wedding."

"And here comes my husband," she said as Ivor approached in a leisurely manner, carrying both a smile and a box under his arm.

"My first pair of shoes," he said, "and I must say I do like them."

He opened the box to show a plain pair of off-white men's shoes. "They will be perfect with those jazzy socks." Ivor smiled at Vivienne.

"And I've got the perfect shoes and a matching headdress," said Vivienne. "Look, they are rose-coloured, the same colour as the bodice of my dress and those flared sleeves."

"And here is madam's headdress," added the assistant, taking the delicate froth of net with the rose out of its box.

"Vivienne, I won't know you either," said Ivor with a smile.

They waited whilst the assistant wrote up the accounts and then Ivor paid with his bank card. Two contented people left the shop.

"Now for that lunch I promised us ... in the café that keeps my paintings," said Ivor. "Just hang onto those boxes. I am glad we have what we need and I don't want to repeat that in a hurry..."

Arm in arm, they walked together up the street until they reached Café Excel with the paintings. The aromatic smells of food cooking tickled their noses.

They entered the shop, talking and smiling and the café owner Charles Jenkins came forward immediately to greet them. His dark eyes smiled behind his glasses.

"Ivor the artist," he said fervently. "How good to see you. The last time I saw you, you were marrying this good woman. And to think you met her in my café."

"That's why I invited you, Charlie," said Ivor. "You were integral to this happy union." He gave Vivienne an affectionate hug. "This place feels like home." Ivor looked around. "Charlie, you and this place helped me get on my feet here. You found me the house I am in and keep my paintings and sell them. You are a good friend."

"Yes, you've been so good to Ivor, Charlie. I'm really glad you were able to come to our wedding," said Vivienne.

"Oh, I am, too," said Ivor. "It was good of you to travel all the way to Rooi Els for the ceremony."

Charlie Jenkins smiled. "I wouldn't have missed it for the world."

They sat at a table by the window, with a white cloth on it and a few flowers in a vase.

"I'm going to have what I had last time," said Vivienne. "Shellfish soup with homemade hot brown bread with lots of butter."

"You're making me hungry," said Ivor, "but I'll go for a cheese lasagne. Charlie, here, makes wonderful spinach lasagne with thick cheese sauce."

"You're making me hungry too," said Vivienne, "but I'll stick with that wonderful flavoursome soup."

"I would like another two paintings from you, Ivor," said Charlie. "What sells well are scenes of water and rocks, I guess because Kalk Bay is on the shores of False Bay."

"Right, I'll look in my gallery at home," said Ivor. "I have a large collection of framed paintings."

Vivienne nodded. "Oh, yes, he does. His lounge is full of them."

"Thank you. Your order won't be long," said Charlie. "Perhaps a coffee meantime?"

"Oh yes," said Ivor, "a cappuccino for me and for you, Vivienne?

"The same," she said.

"Meantime, can we look at the paintings?" Vivienne asked Charlie. "I did enjoy your wide variety of paintings."

"Yes, certainly," said Charlie with a big smile.

"Have you ever thought of including photographic scenes?" asked Vivienne, thinking of Julie's dramatic photography.

"No, but I'm not adverse to the idea," said Charlie.

"I have a friend in Rooi Els with a photographic studio and she has amazing dramatic black-and-white pictures that I am sure your customers would love."

"Was she also at your wedding?"

"Yes," said Vivienne. "The pretty young woman with long golden hair and blue eyes."

"I remember seeing her. Please ask her if she would let me have say three big artistic photographs black and white with backlighting."

"That's what she specializes in," said Vivienne.

"When will you be seeing her?"

"I'm not sure. We sometimes go on days out to paint, but these days we have been a bit busy."

"We did go there a week or so ago when Curly painted so well," said Ivor, "and maybe we can go again and take Walter."

"That would be great," said Vivienne.

"Well, your food will be here in a few minutes if you want to take a quick look around at my latest exhibits."

So Vivienne and Ivor, leaving their packages under the table, did a fairly quick walk around looking at what was new.

"Penguins, look at them," said Vivienne. "Aren't they cute?"

"And look at this one of Bird Island with the birds nesting," said Ivor. "You have some interesting paintings, Charlie."

"Your food has arrived," said Charlie, "and it's good to eat it while it's hot."

So Ivor and Vivienne returned to the bar counter. Vivienne smiled as she saw more jars of preserved figs. She didn't tell Ivor her first purchase had done well as a sling when a boy had tried to rob her and she had swung her bag with the jar of figs in it, and knocked him over.

That was in the past, but it did cross her mind and she smiled.

Ivor was already enjoying his lasagne. "Come, Vivienne, your soup is beautifully hot."

Vivienne nodded and seated herself opposite Ivor. She ate the thick brown bread with butter first, followed by spoonful's of delicious full- flavoured soup."

"Well, I'll need a sleep when we get home," said Ivor. "It's been a good day."

"Yes, it has," agreed Vivienne.

Back at the house, both Ivor and Vivienne laid down on their king-size bed to rest. Ivor put his arms around Vivienne. "What I've been missing in life," he said. "To have a warm comforting wife to hold in my arms. The joy of it." He bent and kissed her, his beard gently tickling her face.

Vivienne snuggled closer to him. She was happier than she was when she was painting and soon they were both asleep.

They slept for about an hour, long deep comforting sleep until the jarring sound of Ivor's cell phone woke them up.

It was Walter.

"Oh, not again," whispered Vivienne.

"Now what is it, Walter?" asked Ivor switching on the speaker so Vivienne could hear.

"It's Cecile again," breathed Walter. "I had a beautiful peaceful night after our painting and even did some lovely paintings in the evening. Fortunately, she doesn't know where I am staying, but she knows where my hardware shop is and visited me there. I won't say visited. I will say created a scene. Luckily, there were no customers at the time, but she saw Rose there and threw a tantrum. Rose was very professional and self-contained and didn't react, but this is just too much, Ivor."

"Stay calm, Walter," Ivor said. You have made big strides and, of course, Cecile doesn't like it, but that is her problem.. Please don't overreact. Please, Walter. Be calm and don't talk back. Let her rant. I know it's not easy, but it's going to harm you if you get involved with her ranting."

"It's difficult to stay calm," said Walter.

"Of course, it is," said Ivor. "But that will bring you out of the woods quicker than anything else ... she can't stay forever in your shop. She will leave. Just see she doesn't follow you to your bed and breakfast. Just don't talk to her. Don't answer back. Don't justify. You have made great strides in making some time in which to paint. Now keep that time to paint in and, by the way, would you like to join us in a couple of days at Rooi Els to paint ... Vivienne's friend won't mind if we go there again, as we want to see if she will let my little café that keeps my paintings also keep a few of her photographs. She has such an eye for the drama in black and white with backlighting. Delightful work."

"Yes, I'd love that," said Walter. "And this time I'll leave Rose in charge of the shop. I do have a car and will drive there myself."

"And Curly has that big motorbike. We need just to see it is alright for Julie and Curly and we'll have our final dress rehearsal before the big day next weekend."

"Have you checked out the venue," asked Walter.

"No," said Ivor, "but Vivienne and I will do that tomorrow after finishing in the studio. Won't we, Vivienne?"

"Yes, it is on my list of things to do and what do you think, Ivor, if we ask them if they can play "Four Seasons" by Vivaldi, whilst people are viewing. You will have your four seasons there, won't you?"

"Vivienne, how did I manage without you," said Ivor. "You are full of wonderful ideas. Yes, we will ask them if they don't mind."

~~~

The venue for the art exhibition was in a quiet part of town, in a building that had a wide-open area on the ground level with trees on both sides and nicely mowed lawn in the middle. Small shrubs and flowering plants were the trimmings at the end of the lawn. Centre of attraction was a mini- waterfall and fish pond with large koi fish swimming lazily around. All of this led into a large tiled foyer, which was to be the Exhibition Centre. Around it were benches on which people could sit and small tables in case the person chose to eat or drink anything.

Leading off this exhibition area were twelve doors leading to twelve different rooms, each to host a different skill. The creators of the exhibition wanted to encourage entrepreneurship amongst people and aimed to help people to start businesses. One example would be the artists leading up to completed paintings and to a gallery where their paintings were sold. The idea was to show especially young people different ways their entrepreneurship could go. There was to be a baking section where the young people would show off how they made and baked cakes and then decorated the cooled cakes. These could then go into a shop of their own where they sold cakes and other good things to eat. Another, was a sports centre where the young people had a room to display their ability to play table tennis. Then how this could lead to running clubs where people came to enjoy themselves and then the best would enter competitions in different parts of the country.

This could lead to earning an income through focus on one particular sport. There was a shop showing knitwear where people using knitting machines easily made beautiful woollen coats and dresses, as well as blankets and baby clothes. These, too, could become a business in a shop, or otherwise, sold through online advertising. Another was a women's boutique with lovely dresses for women, created by two young women who would sew for people to watch. The lovely dresses could become items in a specialist shop or be sold to businesses already running or again, sold on line. Another popular one was teen wear for both genders with two people busily creating styles young people would love to wear.

This big venue with its dozen large exhibition rooms leading off it also had a café where people could get refreshments.

Vivienne got quite excited. "Ivor, this is a marvellous concept," she said. "You show people how they start by learning to paint, and quickly by practice get to a stage where they can market their paintings. Originals signed by them, and then they can choose backings and frames and put them into galleries of their own. Or into other people's galleries." Vivien was excited and said to Ivor, "You should have a gallery of your own."

"You mean, of our own."

"Well. Yes, our own," said Vivienne. "I might be able to exhibit paintings I do, especially of the sky and the sea."

"It's an idea we can think about," said Ivor. "But for now let's see how our room is laid out."

The exhibition member showed Ivor their room. "Number 7," he said.

"That's a nice number," said Vivienne. "Let's look inside."

"Yes, there's ample room for visitors to walk around the room." Four trestle tables were spaced at wide intervals.

"One each," said Ivor. "And there's a small table next to each where we can place our painting materials."

Do they have a plug so we could play Vivaldi music?" asked Vivienne. "Let's ask if they mind."

"I think the room is big enough to muffle the sound so it would not worry people visiting other venues," said Ivor. "We can play it off our cell phones, but playing it off a CD on a CD player would give better sound. But as you say, we do need a plug. "

"Yes," said Vivienne, "but luckily there are several plug points around the room so it is nicely equipped."

"And it has a lock, so we can lock it at lunch time, if we all feel we need to be out of it at the same time."

"Very good," said Vivienne.

"Now we have to see if Curly is available for a dress rehearsal and if Julie would allow us to do our painting on her creative property and also if she would like to exhibit in Charlie Jenkin's gallery."

"Yes, all of that," said Ivor. "All very exciting."

But Vivienne was worried. "I still have to find out about visas to Paris."

"Not now," said Ivor "That can be tomorrow's job. Let's finish properly here."

"How do people pay to enter and what do we need to pay to run our exhibition?"

"Your big paintings will be outside in the hall," said Vivienne. "I think that is important to attract people to want to see us painting."

"Yes, two on either side, one above the other on both sides. So your eye travels from spring to summer to autumn and then to winter. Let's find the organisers and make final arrangements. And pay whatever we have to pay."

The hosts answered all Ivor's questions. Satisfied they would be well- organized and that guests could relax and eat and take their time visiting the various entrepreneurial venues, Ivor and Vivienne returned home.

"I'm exhausted," said Ivor. "It was exhausting to walk around those large venues to get all the information we need."

"But it's done," said Vivienne. "Now we concentrate on our next mission."

"Which is the visit to France," said Ivor.

"Yes, I have looked at their website and see that there is likely to be an easier time for us as we are on a family visit ... a wedding ... and the bride in question is French. So maybe this will hasten it all for us."

"Good," said Ivor. "For now, let's sit in the lounge and relax. Do nothing, or continue chatting about our lives."

"Alright," said Vivienne. "A quick supper and I have the snacks you enjoy ... glacé fruit and cheesy nibbles, so let's take a glass of wine each and enjoy being by ourselves."

"Agreed," said Ivor. "I love having my wife to myself." He gave her an affectionate hug.

Vivienne responded, noticing a lot of stress leaving them with the hug they gave each other.

Ivor looked at Vivienne, "We are doing fine, don't you think, Vivienne?"

"For a newly married couple, I think we are exceptional," replied Vivienne with a smile. "Please amuse yourself for fifteen minutes, while I fix us a quick supper then we can relax."

Half an hour later, Ivor helped Vivienne with the collection of nibbles she had put out for them. Taking their wine, they relaxed on the sofa in the lounge. Both did similar things. Let out a huge big sigh, then relaxed in the cushions of the sofa, and smiled at one another.

"Cheers to success every day," said Ivor, clinking his glass against Vivienne's.

"Yes, daily success," she said, adding, "There are your favourite glace melon, Ivor. Please help yourself."

"Thank you, I will," said Ivor, adding, "I was so enjoying listening to you talk about your early life. You must have got married early to have Steven, who is now thirty-five I think you said."

"Oh yes, I met Paul during teacher training and we married in my last year of training. Steven was born early the next year and I had to take maternity leave after just starting as a teacher.

My mother was alive then and she looked after Steven in the mornings once I went back to teach and I took over in the afternoon. It was exhausting, but I managed.

"Then after a couple of years in a government school, Paul got a lovely post at a boy's private school in the country, actually in the midlands. I didn't teach then, except for some locum work when teachers went on leave or were off sick. That's where I learnt my bit of drawing ... from the art teacher at Cransville Junior School. I was a good housewife ... I looked after Steven, who was not yet at school, cooked for Steven and Paul, bottled fruit, experimented with new recipes, did some gardening and helped with extra-mural English lessons.

"Paul passed away unexpectedly after we had been there for quite a number of years. He got a very good pension package and Steven helped me to relocate to Cowies Hill and to select the house I bought. He was just fifteen years old at that time and had enjoyed his education in the country.

"And that's when you got a post at a girls' finishing school?"

"Yes," said Vivienne, "and that story can wait for another night." She took Ivor's hands in hers and squeezed them, "Now is your turn," she said firmly.

"Vivienne, I've told you a lot about my roaming about the world painting. Imagine it, these sandals, loose baggy pants, checked shirts."

"With missing buttons," said Vivienne.

"Always clean, but maybe missing a button or two," admitted Ivor. "And, of course, my loose overcoat. It has a twenty-year guarantee. It's great to keep out the cold and the heat and I wouldn't be without it."

"Except for at Steven's wedding," said Vivienne with a little amused smile.

"Yes, of course, and I did enjoy that adventure," he said. "Something new for me."

"And your young life?"

"Vivienne, I can't remember anything. Nothing at all. But Lady Lavender helped to unearth bits but I'd rather not go into that for now. Some of it is painful and this has been such a pleasant day."

And he turned and hugged Vivienne and kissed her, lingering as he did.

Vivienne responded. How full and joyous her life had become! Staying in the moment is pretty good, she briefly thought to herself, laughing a bit.

"My dear wife, why the mirth?" asked Ivor.

"Oh Ivor, I was just thinking how wonderful life is with you," Vivienne responded truthfully. "And how good each moment is."

Ivor clearly knew what she meant, because he gave her an extra hug.

"Dearest, Vivienne, how I appreciate you and your lovely energy," said Ivor.

"Thank you, Ivor, and likewise, I appreciate you and your energy with which you paint and live life," she said.

They smiled at one another and Vivienne said, "Mutual admiration, eh, Ivor?"

"True," he said. "Anyway, I'm happy with life, but will be glad when my exhibition is over and we have all our documents in order for our visit to Paris. It will be quick … just a few days … as now I have new students after the exhibition and I don't want them to go cold as it were ... and lose interest."

"I quite understand," said Vivienne. "Steven will be busy with his work, the new baby and Mariette, so staying longer wouldn't mean I'd get to see more of him." She smiled at Ivor and held his hand again. "I'm happy with my new life and with you, Ivor. I love your teasing and your warmth and big bear hugs..."

# Chapter 8

Ivor was preparing to go to the studio on his own,

"It's best if I stay here and get all this paperwork sorted out," said Vivienne. "Phoning them is the best and that's should be done early."

"Right, I'll leave you to it," said Ivor, giving her a quick kiss and then walking in his usual leisurely way out of the kitchen back door and down the stairs.

After tidying the kitchen, Vivienne went to the dining room where she had pages of paper on the table. She knew to get the visas they needed to make a personal visit for both of them to the Cape Town embassy for Paris.

But first she made a phone call and explained her mission and need for visas. It seemed they did have an advantage. It was family business, a wedding, and she was mother of the groom, and Ivor, stepfather. An added advantage was that her son was marrying a French young lady.

"But you and your husband need to come in as soon as possible," said the assistant. "Tomorrow ... you need to make a cash payment so please bring cash with you."

"There are many documents to fill in and you cannot make a mistake. However, we will help you do all this correctly."

Vivienne knew that the passport office also required a personal visit and a payment in cash, but the process was easier.

Vivienne felt quite exhausted by lunch time when Ivor was back from the studio. However, he was pleased with her progress and agreed that the next day he would draw cash and they would go together with their identity documents to get the paperwork done as soon as possible.

"I feel quite stressed," said Vivienne, "and will only feel better once we have filled in everything and supplied the required photos and paid the required amount."

"Tomorrow," said Ivor. "So don't think about it again. We need to maybe get some sea air and relax down at the harbour."

"Or visit Lady Lavender."

"No, I don't think so," said Ivor. "Just a peaceful hour or two maybe walking on the beach and just doing nothing."

"Sounds good," said Vivienne.

"Today is still today and so grab your windcheater, Vivienne, there's always a breeze down at the water's edge."

It was a lovely idea and they walked there, arm in arm, Vivienne remembering to be aware of the moment with the sight of the waves as they lazily broke against the shore, the deep-blue of the endless vista of False Bay with the misty mountains on the other side.

"Somewhere along that shore is Rooi Els," said Vivienne.

"True," said Ivor. "And we are having a busy time, with a visit to the great city tomorrow. We still have the painting rehearsal and did you check with Julie?"

"Yes, and she's happy. Any weekday is fine for her," said Vivienne adding, "and did you check with Curly?"

"I did," said Ivor, "and as he is retired, likewise, any day suits."

"So we just have to decide on a day and let our small team know," said Vivienne. "It's all rather fun, isn't it?"

"Yes, it is," said Ivor. "Fun with an outcome … to be able to paint in front of visitors, who will watch you and maybe ask questions."

"Don't scare me," said Vivienne.

"It's not scaring you, Vivienne, it's just preparing you. Maybe I wander about between the three of you and ask questions"

Vivienne laughed. "Yes, let's rather all paint at the outdoor tables in Julie's outdoor refreshment area. We can all just paint from memory."

"Yes, that's great. We really don't need to go all the way to Rooi Els to do that, though."

"But it has such a creative atmosphere," said Vivienne. "The mountains that speak to us and the heathers and heaths. And the baboons that roam around. It will always be a very special spot for me, that place," said Vivienne. "Your painting course meant so much to me."

Ivor laughed. "With reservations, Vivienne," he said. "Have you forgotten Maureen and the scene she made?"

"No, I haven't," said Vivienne.

"But," said Ivor. "You were the great benefit I had."

"I was getting to know you better, Ivor. We wouldn't be where we are today without that amazing week together."

Ivor looked at Vivienne, his hazel eyes twinkling. "Oh yes, that was the best decision I ever made … to ask you to come with me."

Vivienne remembered and laughed. "You told me it wasn't just the coffee… and it wasn't."

They spent another fifteen minutes wandering about on the sands, arm in arm. The wind blew Vivienne's hair and she pushed it out of her eyes. She was more content than she had ever been. Such beauty of the sea and with the man she loved with her.

The wind had sharpened and Ivor drew his big loose coat tightly around him. Vivienne, who had noticed, zipped up her windcheater and said to Ivor with a smile, "Your special coat keeps you warm."

"Oh yes, cool and warm. But it's getting chilly so let's make our way back home. Being there is better even than my precious coat."

Vivienne laughed and took his arm as they hurried home.

Tomorrow they would go to Cape Town and deal with all the paperwork for their Paris trip making sure that every detail was attended to.

And on the following day they did exactly that. They attended to all the paperwork in the Cape Town offices and paid the required fees. All would now be in order for their Paris visit. They could now concentrate on their impending painting rehearsal and then the exhibition.

~~~

It was the day of their painting rehearsal. In less than a week the exhibition would take place. So, though this was fun, it was also serious. Walter had taken his car from his garage at home, with he said, a lot of abuse hurled at him by Cecile, but he had taken it anyway. He had arranged to pick up Curly and they arrived at Julie's place just after Ivor and Vivienne had arrived.

Julie, with her flowing golden hair and sparkling blue eyes was out to meet Ivor and Vivienne, giving them each a big bear hug.

"This is such a lovely idea," she said. "And it's so nice of you to let me paint with you. I'll visit you at the exhibition, though, and watch you paint there, too." She chuckled at the idea.

"Don't rub it in," said Vivienne. "Today, is our rehearsal and Ivor said he would act like the public and wander amongst our tables and watch us paint."

The refreshment area was large and shady with a view down to the sea through the greenery of plants and shrubs. There were five large outdoor tables, each with its own umbrella and a few chairs. The area was fenced with two gates leading into the forested area and down to the sea.

"I haven't unlocked them today," said Julie, "as the intention is to stay up here and paint, isn't that so?"

"Correct," said Ivor. "We will be finished by lunchtime, so let's get started."

"There's a tap over there in case you need it for your water jars," said Julie, "and let me get my painting equipment then I'll be ready to join you."

Vivienne greeted both Walter and Curly. She was glad to notice that Walter looked a lot more relaxed and at ease than he had done the last time they were here. And Curly had his usual smile in a slim face under a bald head.

"The name Curly is such a misnomer." Vivienne asked him, "Curly, where did your nickname come from.?"

"Oh, it goes back a long way," said Curly, "to when I was a small boy and had a mass of curly blond hair. It was a school nickname and it stuck."

Vivienne laughed. "I like it, but it doesn't exactly describe you now."

"No, it's fashionable to have no hair," he said. "But I like being called Curly. So the nickname stuck."

"And, Walter, you look so much better," said Vivienne.

"Yes I've been doing my best to keep my mind off my problems. I'm occupied in my shop in the day, and get back to eat at this nice bed and breakfast. Then painting every night," he said, "and going to sleep only when I am really tired, and sleeping well."

"And Cecile?"

"Cecile can decide what she wants to do," said Walter. "Without me. Rose is not important at the moment. She helps in my shop, but it's more important for me to get myself on an even keel and this painting is helping me with that."

"All good," said Vivienne.

"Come now, everyone, please get yourself organized at any table that you like," said Ivor. "We are making this a relaxed session just as it will be at the Exhibition Centre. There is will be a small table next to each larger table on which you will paint. You can store your art materials on the small table so we don't look cluttered. And you can wear any clothing you like. Arty is good, I suggest."

In minutes, all had settled. "Do we wait for you to tell us when to start?" asked Curly.

"No, I don't think so," said Ivor. "We want to appear natural and relaxed so just start as you wish. You all have brought your own materials, which will be the same as you take with you on Saturday."

Vivienne watched as the artists organized themselves in an individual way.

"And we paint anything?" asked Walter.

"Yes, anything," said Ivor. "From your imagination. This is creative watercolour painting. Remember you have learnt how to paint misty mornings, with softly fading trees in the background and well-defined ones in the front. You can paint water with reflections. Distant mountains, the sea. A landscape with a sandy path and trees. Could be summer or winter . The colouring will be very different. Each decide what it was that you want to paint and we'll stop in an hour and a half.

"By the way, I've brought a music player along and will play Vivaldi's "Four Seasons" while you paint."

They all smiled at Ivor.

"Wonderful idea," said Julie. "You can very faintly hear the sea here but the music will disguise it."

"Would you prefer the sea?" asked Ivor.

"No," said Julie. "I was just mentioning it … the sound of the sea is inspiring for me. But I'm happy to paint to music today."

"We want to have this music playing at the Exhibition Centre," explained Vivienne. "So, this is our practice."

Ivor had turned on the music player and the first strains of vibrant spring was playing.

Walter pushed his hair back and laughed. "You can't know how rejuvenating this is for me," he said. "I'm all for music and I'll be into something exciting very soon."

There were a few more comments and then Vivienne noticed all four were in their own worlds, heads low, palettes out and artists were bobbing paint onto their pallets.

"Please bring spotlessly clean palettes on Saturday," said Ivor. "I know in no time at all they are a mess with all the colours, as you add water to them and they spread and mix."

No one spoke, but heads nodded. No one wanted to talk as the creative juices had started to flow. Vivaldi's music played and Julia said, "I can still faintly hear the sea."

"Shall I increase the volume," asked Ivor.

"Yes please," said Julie. "I hear the sea every day all the time and this music is something different."

Ivor put up the volume, and Vivienne sat with her eyes shut, just listening to the music. Above them, the mountain loomed. The energies of the plants and animal life whispered to her. She sat just listening to the music and, with a silent mind, soaked up the energies. Soon, she felt she was vibrating on a different much finer level and, yes, with no thoughts inside her head. Her eyes were still shut and the music was playing, soft at times and then louder. Then the music faded out and instead came the desire to squirt blobs of paint onto her palette. She opened her eyes. Her big hake was lying next to her paper, which was steady on a block. She took a deep breath and, without thinking, began to squirt paint out from tubes of paint onto her palette. Not a lot, just the basic colours Ivor had taught them to use. Ultramarine blue, raw sienna, lemon-yellow, alizarin-crimson, paynes grey, burnt umber, and indigo.

Amazingly, she found her brush just dipping itself into the paint. It was all done without effort ... she remembered Ivor saying painting with effort is not painting. You are to relax and let the paint and brush take over... make it effortless.

Vivienne smiled. So far it had been effortless, but what was to go in the lower two thirds of the paper? Obviously, the dominant part of her painting was in the lower part as the sky line was high, about a third of the way down. What was her hake to select next? It spread strokes of water across her page. Then it dipped into raw sienna and rapid stokes with the hake filled up the top third of her paper. Now the brush dipped itself into water to clean off the yellow and selected the ultramarine and soon, thereafter, there were swirling white clouds tinged with sunlight, floating around in a blue sky. A touch of alizarin crimson gave warmth to the sky.

In less than ten minutes the sky was complete. Vivienne took a breath and looked at what she had done. Obviously, the sky was not the dominant feature as it occupied the top third of the paper with swirling white clouds, tinged with sunlight, floating in a serene blue sky. What was to go in the bottom two-thirds? There was still plenty of time and she didn't know… which she thought was just as well.

But all the same she closed her eyes again and listened to the music. She didn't sit like that for long as she opened her eyes and again washed her paper with water below the horizon, stopping a little above the bottom of the paper. Obviously, some soft wet into wet, she thought, as the brush mixed on the paper some blue and yellow to make a soft misty green and into it went some slightly darker green, which also turned misty on the damp paper. Distant trees, she silently thought, as her brush went into blue and painted a river twisting through the trees. a river with definition as it broadened onto the dry part of the paper, and formed a wide river. She had some trees and shrubs and rocks on the shores and these reflected in the water with small white bits of paper looking like foamy bits where the water went over rocks.

The scene on either side were different. On the one side was the hint of a large hill and, on the other, flat green grassland with clumps of red and yellow flowers. "Don't fiddle," Ivor had said. And had also warned, "Stop before you think you have finished."

Vivienne had spent a long time with the misty trees and the swirling blue river, the rocks and flowers and trees and her hour and a half was almost up. Maybe I could do more, but I think I'll stop. She gave a big sigh of relief, as though she was supposed to be relaxing. She had been tense, especially as Ivor had been wandering between the tables and looking at what his artists were doing.

But he smiled at Vivienne as she put down her brush. "Tough work, Vivienne," he said, "but well done. I'm sure you are pleased with what you have done. And would you like to walk around with me and look at what our other artists have done? It won't phase them as this is going to happen next Saturday and what is more the people looking are likely to talk to the artist so be prepared for interruptions."

So Ivor and Vivienne walked around. Vivienne was amazed to see how different each artist's work was. Walter had been energetic with a lot of reds and oranges, a sky with a boat on a lake and twisty dark trees bending over. Curly had gone for a mountain scene with emphasis on the rocky nature of the mountain, with its clothing of green bushes in contrast with the dark rocks and sandy path leading up the mountainside.

And Julie had painted the sea and had put in a mermaid, "This is me," she said with a smile when Vivienne and Ivor looked at it. "Remember you thought I was a mermaid. And so I have brought her to life."

"Very satisfactory all round," said Ivor, pleased, and smiling, shoulder-length brown hair glinting in the sunlight.

"And," said Julie, "the lunch is ready. Pizzas of various combinations, I hope you are okay with that."

The aroma of the pizzas as the waiter brought them through took Vivienne's thoughts off painting to the delicious treat awaiting them.

"And there is a selection of desserts after," said Julie. "Something sweet is always nice after something savoury."

Soon they were all seated at the sixth large table and easy conversation took place.

"No need to worry about your part in the exhibition," said Ivor. "Just do exactly what you did today, but painting something different is a good idea and thank you all for your participation."

The thanks were returned as all felt the time was wonderfully spent – in nature with music and the energies of mountains, the sea and the green covering, with birds and the occasional baboon.

"So I'll see you at nine o clock sharp on Saturday at the exhibition centre; and thank you all most sincerely."

Vivienne looked at him. He was serious as this was all-important to him, though he had wanted them to be casual.

While Ivor was talking to Julie and Walter and Curly were talking to one another, Vivienne stayed silent. The mountain towered behind her and the sea in front was faintly audible. Around her was green vegetation, with birds in the sky. She was aware of where she was and her joy at being there. Her no-thought head suddenly brought in Lady Lavender. Lady Lavender, who was pleased with the way Vivienne was controlling her thoughts and staying in the moment. Lady Lavender, who had told her one mission for her was to be a support for Ivor, who had in his early life been badly stunted … he needed to flourish and grow as he had a mission and that was to develop artists, who used pure energy in their work that would uplift and cheer people greatly.

She smiled to herself. Today, was what Lady Lavender had meant for Ivor. His students had been confident and very creative. Vivienne had a good feeling about the exhibition … now only a few days away.

Vivienne was also glad that Ivor had remembered to ask Julie if she would be interested in letting him take back three of her backlit black and white mounted photographs to put in Charlie Jenkin's studio. Vivienne was in time to see Julie handing the framed photographs to Ivor and saying in delight, "What a big thing this will be for me. To have my photographs in an art shop in Kalk Bay! I'm thrilled and thanks so much Ivor." And Vivienne watched as Ivor carefully placed them in the boot of his car.

Time went past quickly and it was the day of the exhibition. Vivienne checked with herself. No need to take anything to eat or drink. There was a café there and there would be vending machines to buy still water to drink. But it was important that she had everything she might need for herself as an artist painting in view of the public.

All her art materials were in a big basket, and everything was in order. Ivor had a music player with a CD of Vivaldi's Four Season's in it.

Now to check her own clothing. A warm jacket in case the weather changed or the air-conditioners were on and were too cool. And what to wear?

Ivor had told them to dress as artists. She discarded the idea of a dress. Jeans with an arty shirt would be ideal. She selected one that wasn't quite gaudy, but nearly there. It had great splashes of various colours. Red, yellow, green, blue, purple and deep-grey. She loved the material. It was crease-resistant and of a heavy kind of silk and it felt good when she wore it. Perhaps a beret on her head. What colour? A nice deep-rose. Funny, she thought, those are the colours of my outfit for Steven's wedding.

She brushed her bobbed dark hair and applied minimal makeup. The effect when she added the deep-rose beret was arty. Her deep-blue eyes had an unusual sparkle in them.

I'm going to enjoy today, she thought, and knew that this was the best thing she could do for Ivor. Be relaxed and happy.

She checked on Ivor, who was looking serious. He, too, was making an attempt to look a bit more arty than usual and had on tan baggy trousers with a deep-blue shirt and, of course, the usual artist's loose jacket. When he saw her he lightened up and smiled.

"Oh, my artist wife," he said. "Come here dearest one, let's give one another a good morning hug." Vivienne was quickly in his arms and enjoying his bear like hug. Resting against his chest, she said, "I could stay like this forever."

"And miss the exhibition?" asked Ivor, in mock horror. "My prime student not there to show visitors how splendid it is to immerse oneself in the world of paint …"

Vivienne laughed and released herself from his hold.

"No, Ivor, I would not miss that exhibition for anything. Have you got everything you need? The music player?"

"Oh, yes," said Ivor. "And my painting equipment as I'll be painting too."

"Then let's go," said Vivienne.

When they arrived at the large parking area that ran on three sides of the lawn there were already a number of cars there. It wasn't far to walk with their equipment and Vivienne laughed as they stopped at the fishpond and waterfall. The water splashed down gently into the pond with water plants and orange and grey large koi fish swimming around.

"Those koi fish that keep opening their mouths look like they are talking to us," she said.

"Maybe they are wishing us well," said Ivor.

"Oh yes, could be," said Vivienne as they walked on and arrived at the exhibition hall with its black-and-white tiled floor. Already there were a number of people inside and Ivor and Vivienne checked their tickets with the security guard at the entrance.

Vivienne's eyes went straight to Venue 7, with four large framed watercolour paintings announcing an artist's entrepreneurial exhibition. Two were on either side, one above the other and, indeed, they were eye-catching.

Vivienne noticed that at each door the exhibitions announced what they were showing with posters of baking, knitwear, designer clothes, toddler outfits and teen styles. And at the centre back, were posters of food, denoting the café area. Already the smells of hot rolls and boerewors tickled her sense-buds.

"Making me hungry," she whispered to Ivor.

"Not so early, Vivienne," said Ivor with a laugh. "You have to earn your treat. Like little Tommy Tucker who sang for his supper. You have to paint for your taskmaster."

"You are such a hard taskmaster," Vivienne joked back, as they both entered their venue and took stock.

The four large tables were covered in white plastic table cloths. It seemed to be waiting for them to liven it up. At that moment,

Walter and Curly arrived, both laughing, which was a good sign. No one was nervous.

"When do we start painting?" asked Curly.

"Just as soon as you are settled," said Ivor. "Don't rush … and paint as many paintings as you like. There is a railing all around the walls and you can stand your finished paintings on those. It will make the room look most attractive. And you can go out for a tea break whenever you feel like it. Vivienne feels like it right now, don't you. Vivienne?"

"Oh yes, the food smells make me hungry, but I'll do what Ivor suggests… paint first and eat afterwards."

"And the lunch break encourages you to talk to others who are here. There are tables outside next to the benches. Network. And I'll settle first and then put on the music… we will have an atmosphere all of our own."

Looking up, Vivienne smiled. Three heads were intently bent over as each got organized to paint. Walter was the first, she noticed, to use his large hake brush and to paint in a blue sky with white drifting clouds, Curly was hesitating, but Ivor was already putting masterful strokes of red onto his watercolour paper. Vivienne didn't stop to see what came next as she was busy with her own creation, today, a pale background with large poppies softly emerging from the background. She had recently introduced herself to flower painting and was pleased with the result.

A voice next to her said, "I really like that and you've done it so quickly." She looked up at the face of an elderly woman.

Vivienne replied honestly. "I've only just discovered flower painting," she said. "I thought it would be difficult but it's not. It's a lot of fun."

"I wonder if I am too old to learn to paint," said the woman. "I'm Priscilla, by the way."

"Vivienne," said Vivienne. Not attempting to shake hands as her hake was mid-air, said, "No age is too old. Please give your name and details to my husband, Ivor, himself a great artist." She indicated Ivor.

"Don't let me stop you," said the woman. "I'm interested in the other artists too." She nodded to Vivienne and moved on.

Vivienne noticed that there were now a number of people walking around, watching the artists. She was glad they were all so well-prepared and confident, applying paint rapidly to their boards. Another man hesitated next to Vivienne. He too liked her loose poppies that melted into a background. "Nice loose work," he said. "I'm interested in painting. Never tried it myself, though."

Vivienne smiled at him. "Why not?" she said. "My husband is collecting names of those who'd like to become students. You will be glad you enrolled." The man nodded and walked on. Vivienne could see small groups of people at each artist's table and wondered how they would cope with the interruptions.

It doesn't matter, she told herself. Just relax and have fun and let the brush decide what to paint.

It wasn't long before each of them had finished one painting and put it on the ledge that ran around the room and had started on another. Interest in the artists was growing. And, at one point, Ivor stopped the music, and spoke to the large crowd of people now in his venue.

"You couldn't do anything better than learn watercolour painting with the hake," and he showed his big brush. "It rapidly puts down paint so that paintings get done easily and quickly. It stops the inclination to fiddle and the results are clean and exciting ... note what my artists have done in this past hour .., already there are eleven paintings around the room." There were appreciative murmurs from the onlookers.

"And, with practice, you can soon frame them and sell them. There is a good market for original creative watercolours. If you are interested, please talk to me at the break and leave your contact details for me to get in touch with you. I will be running a new course in the next couple of weeks."

The energy in the room was warm and positive and uplifting. Vivienne could feel it and saw the onlookers smiling. They, too, had encountered the positive feelings these artists gave off as they painted.

Very soon it was time for lunch and Ivor watched as the last person went out then he shut and locked the door.

"Artists, we have a forty-five-minute break," he said. "Enjoy your lunch and speak to people. There are other entrepreneurial activities going on so we have lots of competition."

He nodded towards the other doors with people coming out of them.

At lunch time, Vivienne noticed a number of people queuing to speak to Ivor. She was glad for him. This would boost his self-confidence.

Someone spoke to her.

It was a well-dressed, middle-aged man. "Do you have your own gallery?" he asked, "because those watercolour paintings outside are outstanding. A gallery with originals of that quality would benefit society. In businesses, doctors' rooms and so on; the tranquillity of those paintings could soothe agitated patients."

"No," said Vivienne, "we don't."

"My name is Simon Merryweather," he said, "and I deal in office property, and could show you an ideal gallery you might like to rent. Your husband could run classes there."

Vivienne smiled. "Wonderful idea." Thank you, Mr Merryweather." She took the card he offered her.

Simon Merryweather nodded to Vivienne. "I might also like to get involved with painting," he said. "I was watching you people paint and you all seemed to be so involved and in love with what you do. No time for worry thoughts." He smiled as he walked on.

No thought, Vivienne thought. No worry thoughts when you paint.

There were many people interested and by closing time at four o'clock, there were some twenty-eight lovely creative watercolour paintings around the room. Ivor took a video of it all.

"I would love to relive this day," he said to Vivienne. "It has been a huge success. And made me and other people happy. "

"I have a surprise for you," said Vivienne.

"Really, dearest wife? Are you going to tell me now or later?"

Vivienne hesitated. "I think later," she said. "We need to talk about it and it's exciting."

Ivor smiled that smile she loved that seemed to disappear into his beard.

"You make me so curious," he said, "but I will have patience and wait until we get home, right, Vivienne?"

"Yes, at home, relaxing with a glass of wine and some nice nibbles ... it needs careful thought."

Walter and Curly were both looking uplifted. Each had painted half a dozen paintings, all different with different colour ranges. Some warm and others cool and misty. Vivienne had a few flower paintings, as she had been trying on her own with large arrangements in vases ... and with flowers growing wild in the field. She had paintings of the sea and one purely of the clouds in the sky, late afternoon with the setting sun tinting the sky with reds, oranges, yellows and some deeper shades of indigo, as night indicated it was getting ready to take over.

Walter thanked the exhibition organizers, who were truly delighted with the artists' entrepreneurial show. "We will promote your work," one of them said. "And it has been successful for people to learn there are many ways to make a living. We had cookery and dressmaking and educational toys. A great day and thank you for your contribution."

At home, after relieving themselves of their artists' materials and having a light supper, Ivor said, "Now for that glass of wine and for us to chill and you to tell me this exciting news."

"I met a man called Simon Merryweather... he is into property for business people and he asked if you have a gallery of your own... suggesting you might like to have one to exhibit your paintings. He was impressed with your spring/summer/autumn/winter paintings and thinks it would benefit professionals like doctors to have a gallery with paintings that are tranquil and can uplift their patients.

"He said you could teach there as well, and I'd say you got a lot of names today."

"I did," said Ivor, "and I'm delighted. I love teaching. Especially with my great friend the hake." They sat together on the sofa in the lounge, relaxed and happy.

Ivor put his arm around Vivienne and turned to look at her. She saw his hazel eyes, serious now as he said, "My darling wife, you have no idea how uplifting this day has been for me and I know a lot of it is to do with having your quiet believing nature with me. I excel. Like the little talk I gave today. I am not a speech-maker but it went down so well and I had a lot of people enlisting to learn to paint."

And he hugged her then kissed her. Vivienne returned the warm kiss that was full of quiet emotion. She too knew today had been a great success.

"So," she said, "is it yes to having a gallery of your own, Ivor?"

He released her. "Yes, dearest wife, it's a big fat yes from me. And you will be involved as well. Your paintings can go on display. When do we meet with Simon Merryweather?"

"Tomorrow afternoon, Ivor. He has given me an address, but I haven't studied it to see where it is. Let me get his card and we can see."

She fetched her big sling bag and rummaged in its interior. Then brought out a card. "This is it," she said, giving it to Ivor.

He studied it and then looked up at Vivienne with a bemused expression on his face.

"Nothing happens by chance," he said. "This shop he is offering us is in this main street and it is only a few shops away from where we live. How blessed can we be? What time do we meet with him, Vivienne?"

"He said to call him. His number is on the card and two-thirty would suit him."

"Thanks," said Ivor. "I'll contact him and tell him we will both be there … and thank him heartily too."

The morning went quickly and, at two-thirty, Ivor and Vivienne closed their front door and went down the stairs to the street below.

Vivienne was laughing.

"I can't believe it's one of those little shops I've looked at so often," she said. "And to think we will be amongst Kalk Bay's creative shopkeepers."

They crossed the little lane and just a few shops up they came to one that was empty.

"This is it," said Ivor, peering into the window. "It shouldn't be long before Mr Merryweather is here."

"I think he's already there," said Vivienne. "Someone has seen us looking in the window and is opening the door."

A smiling smartly dressed middle-aged man greeted them.

"I'm Simon Merryweather," he said. "I recognize Vivienne from yesterday and you must be Ivor the artist?"

"Yes, I am Ivor and Vivienne is my wife. Pleased to meet you, Mr Merryweather."

"Please call me Simon," said the man. "I just know we are going to have a great working relationship. I can't tell you how uplifting I found your four paintings of the four seasons. And I immediately could see them in a gallery of your own where many people pass. And that could happen for you in this shop. Would you like to come inside and see for yourself?"

"Yes, please," said Ivor. He stood aside for Vivienne to enter first.

Simon looked at Vivienne and smiled. "You paint as well?" he asked.

"Yes and she is very good," said Ivor, answering for Vivienne. "Please look around, Vivienne, and see if you feel this is right for us."

Vivienne said without hesitation "Ivor, I know it is. As you said, nothing happens by chance. And this is just a few doors away from where we live. I could easily run this in the morning. And you could still paint in your studio."

"There is also a very large empty room at the back that you could use to teach students," said Simon. "And it is central for students. Even coming by train." He pointed to a train that was zooming along the lines opposite them.

"This is all so inspiring," said Ivor. "I am looking around and this front part could be a showroom for paintings. All standing on easels so people could get a feeling of what each painting would do for them in his office or home. Yes, I like it."

"Maybe we look at the big room at the back?" asked Vivienne.

"There is also a kitchenette and small retirement room at the back," said Simon Merryweather. "So you can be comfortable and also offer customers tea or coffee if you wish."

Ivor and Vivienne smiled at one another. Ivor took her hand. "Let's see the back room for teaching," said Ivor, "and then it's a yes from me."

They followed Simon through the large empty room to a room at the back. The door opened onto a large room with big glass windows letting in plenty of light. It had electricity power points and lights.

"This is perfect for teaching pupils," said Ivor. "What a great idea! Thank you, Simon."

"My pleasure," said Simon Merryweather, looking pleased. "It just hit me yesterday when I saw your uplifting paintings of the four seasons, which displayed here on the main street, would very likely find a grateful buyer. If you are happy, shall we sort out the paper work, now?

"Yes," said Ivor. "This is perfect and thanks for your genius idea."

It didn't take long to sort out the essential details and Ivor and Vivienne returned home, content with the day's activities.

But that wasn't the only idea that Vivienne had had that day. She knew that a visit to Lady Lavender was her mission the next day.

She didn't know why she wanted to visit Lady Lavender other than to thank her for helping her to keep control of her emotions and straying thoughts. But it was more than that she knew.

On knocking on the door of the quaint fisherman's cottage on the beach, a dark eye peered at her through the eye-glass and the door opened to show Lady Lavender in a long dress in shades of lavender and pink.

"Quite charming," she breathed to herself.

Lady Lavender said as she ushered her in, "Quite charming, do you think?"

"It looks beautiful on you," said Vivienne. "It is such lovely material."

"Thank you," said Lady Lavender. "I like it myself. Do come in Vivienne dear and let's head for the kitchen, shall we?"

Shortly afterwards, armed with ginger tea and cinnamon cookies, they repaired to the lounge where Captain was already seated on the big sofa.

"It's good to see you, Vivienne," said Lady Lavender. "I have been keeping track of you and it's nice you have been on an even keel."

"Lady Lavender, I just wanted to thank you for helping me. A lot has happened, all good, and I think we've helped one of Ivor's artist students to get himself on an even keel as you call it."

"I'm so glad, Vivienne, and that you are being able to help Ivor to give maximum help through fine higher energy to students and public alike. Oh, yes, I know about the exhibition. And that it was a success."

Vivienne was taken aback. This is what she had wanted to tell Lady Lavender.

"But," said Lady Lavender, "you have more to tell me, I know."

"Well, an update on the exhibition is that Ivor is leasing a venue of his own on the Main Street where he can exhibit his main paintings and a lot of others he has as well. He has plenty to stock out a venue of his own and he will also be teaching there. And it is about three doors away from where we live so I will be able to help in the mornings."

"All good, Vivienne," said Lady Lavender. "And how do you think Ivor is doing? Is he blossoming?"

Vivienne had to think about that. He had always been rather remote but had changed to a degree.

"I'm not sure about blossoming, Lady Lavender but he is much more open and relaxed," she said. "We talk to one another a lot and he is very affectionate."

"And has he spoken more about his own life?"

"No, he becomes tongue-tied when it comes to that," said Vivienne, "but we are getting on so well. And I am happy, Lady Lavender, more happy than I had ever imagined I would be."

"That's good, Vivienne," said Lady Lavender. "Ivor is a very precious soul with a great gift for humanity and that is his art. His paintings uplift those who see or buy them and, in training new young artists in his own particular style, they too can paint individualistic work that uplift humanity. Very important at this time in history."

"I don't know why I felt it important to come to you today," said Vivienne.

"Maybe just for me to congratulate you and tell you to keep on being Ivor's prop as it were. So that he can carry out his soul's mission. Otherwise, you are on track, Vivienne."

"Yes, we are due to fly to Paris in a week's time to attend Steven's wedding. We won't be away for long, as now Ivor has this new venue and many students. He is keen to start this work."

"I'll be watching over you, Vivienne. Just keep calm and be present and not scattered all over the place and your visit will be a success. I'm honoured you came to visit me, Vivienne, and that all is on track. There are no lectures today, my dear, except to thank you for taking the time to call in on me." She smiled at Vivienne, who felt a great warmth for this strange woman.

Captain had yawned and stood up. Vivienne smiled as she looked at the big cat.

"Time for me to go. Thanks for the reminder, Captain." The big black cat stood up and led the way to the door.

Back at home Vivienne realized that all her worries about the exhibition and its success had been dealt with and the wedding was the next item to deal with. That needed three special presents, and she knew she would find them all in the shops in Main Street. When she hadn't been looking for presents she had seen beautiful items that people would treasure.

Now to revisit those shops and look for something for the baby, a present for the parents and something special for Steven and Marietta. *What would she find?*

The visit to Lady Lavender had taken only half the morning. There was still half of it left. So she started at the bottom of the street, in search of three special presents with no idea of what she was looking for.

The first was a furniture shop. Not anything too big. Anything from it would be too heavy to transport. The next was jewellery, but that was too personal. So beautiful were the items on display, but she bypassed that shop. Next was a shop with first editions of old books and other precious items but nothing there would be suitable.

A knitwear shop was next with all kinds of beautiful knitted garments on show. Stoles, caps, jerseys and a section of baby clothes. How big was Mariette's baby Violet? Was there perhaps something with a violet on it though, of course, the baby was too young to appreciate that. She wandered about amongst the baby ware. Beautiful hand-embroidered dresses, and knitted jumpers and jerseys. It was all too confusing and Vivienne sighed and left feeling depressed. How did one look for a present for a baby when one didn't know the size? She had been born prematurely and was tiny according to Steven. But babies grow very quickly and soon outgrow beautiful clothes.

The next one had linen ware and what she did find was an exquisite large table cloth in fine linen with motifs in the corners of South African scenes, the grand Table Mountain, even False Bay and the coast, with waves and rocks. It was classy and beautiful and Vivienne was delighted. It could do as a present either for the parents or for the young couple. She smiled, picked it up and took it to the counter for the cashier to wrap it and to accept her payment.

"Beautiful, isn't it?" said the assistant as she gift-wrapped it. "I'm surprised it hasn't been sold earlier."

"Well, I'm glad it wasn't," said Vivienne, "because this is an ideal gift to come from South Africa." She left the shop happy, one down and two to go, she thought as she made her way home. She looked forward to telling Ivor of her day's happenings.

At home, she unwrapped the table cloth to show Ivor. "Not everyone uses table cloths these days," she said. "But there are those special occasions when large tables are set with lots of food. I imagine this cloth being used on such an occasion."

"It's a great choice," said Ivor. "For the parents?"

"Yes," said Vivienne. "I'd like to go back tomorrow morning to look around those other charming little shops… something for the baby and for the young couple."

"Fine," said Ivor. "I'll leave you to decide. I'll get on with my latest commission."

So, in the morning Vivienne locked up and was soon much higher up in the street, stopping to gaze into one little shop after another. Lovely musical instruments, old books, and glassware.

Here, she stopped at an antique shop: she hesitated. Then entered. A variety of items asked her to look at them. An old mouth organ, a hammered brass tray and candlesticks to match, a wonderful stinkwood chest. There were the most delicate coloured wine glasses from Murano Glass. Venetian glass, the plaque announced.

There were beautiful alabaster birds, but her eyes went to a set of cut-glass wine glasses. They were set in a small case lined with red silk. She looked at them and could see the young couple and maybe a few friends smiling and toasting one another. Maybe at baby Violet's christening or after their own wedding. They would travel well in that secure little case. And she knew she had found a suitable present for her special son, Steven, and his new young wife-to-be. Vivienne was delighted with her purchase. There was just baby Violet now and she wandered along without thinking and then she saw a tiny jewellery shop. Not much bigger than the door and went inside with no idea of why.

The range of displayed jewellery had her lingering over various rings of all kinds with coloured jewels or simply plain gold. Not a ring ... there were silver bangles and slender gold ones. Beautiful charm bracelets, but not for the baby. Then she saw a lovely pin. With a flower. And the flower was a tiny violet. The pin was of very fine gold and not large. It could be pinned to a baby's dress and it had a little place for a name. Would the name "Violet' fit on there? She was brooding over it when the shopkeeper came to see if he could help.

"I'm looking for a present for a new baby, my first grandchild, actually, and she and her parents live in France. So I haven't seen her yet.

She is too young for this pin, but it is quite charming."

"On the positive side, it will be something she can grow into and wear for years," said the assistant. "And probably keep for ever."

Vivienne looked at it again. It was about an inch-and-a-half long, narrow, with a pin behind and fine gold filigree etching, leaving space for a name. The deciding factor was the small beautiful violet. "Can you engrave the name Violet in that small space," she asked.

"Oh. yes," said the young assistant, "but you will need to come back for it tomorrow."

Vivienne would have loved to take it there and then, to show to Ivor, but to show it to him with the name engraved on it would be even better.

She was immensely happy as she paid for it and made her way home.

Ivor was not in his usual happy frame of mind and Vivienne sensed it immediately.

"What is troubling you, my darling?" she asked him gently. "I've had such a successful day."

"That's great Vivienne. I wonder if we can chat like we were doing … over our lives together."

"Of course," said Vivienne. "Dinner will be ready shortly."

After a meal, when Ivor was unusually silent, they repaired to the lounge each with a glass of red wine.

"Reminds me of the beautiful cut-glass wine glasses I bought today for Steven and Mariette. They are exquisite."

"You need to show them to me … later," said Ivor, still seeming rather distracted.

As they sat together on the comfy sofa, Ivor put his arm round Vivienne. Normally, he was peaceful but today? She looked at him in concern. *What was bothering him?*

Ivor sighed. "Remember I told you I could remember nothing of my childhood? Today, I was painting a scene in which I had a small child and… Today, I need your strength my dear wife."

"Why, Ivor, whatever is the matter?"

"Today, when I was painting an autumn scene with lots of dried and colourful leaves lying in piles, I painted a child sitting amongst the leaves and throwing them up and laughing and a flash-back came into my mind. A vivid flash of myself as a child, not much older than the child I was painting."

"And?" questioned Vivienne to encourage him to go on.

"I remember most vividly also sitting playing in a pile of dried autumn leaves and then getting dreadful news. My mother had died in a car accident. I had a brief flashback of a happy, dark-haired young woman giving me breakfast of a boiled egg when I liked to turn the shell upside-down and hit after I had eaten it. The breakfast I had that morning was the last time I saw my mother, as she died that day."

He was quiet and Vivienne took his hand in hers. At first it was limp and then he tightened his grip as he continued speaking.

"I never really knew my father. He was a boxer and an aggressive man and I had kept away from him. But now he was my sole caretaker and he wasn't very good at it. I remember terrible lumpy porridge and an angry father if I didn't eat it all. I recall that he drank and was often drunk. I was very scared of him and as he didn't make my world a happy place. I had blocked it all from my memory. No loving mom to read me stories and to caress me. Just a sour soulless man who found looking after me a terrible bore. He used his fists to get my attention.

"I don't remember much about school either, other than that I didn't perform well and then at about ten years of age I found I loved painting. Puddling as you call it. I loved art lessons at school.

"I don't think my father knew or cared about me and my love of art until I was about fourteen when the art teacher wouldn't let me paint red clouds. I remember telling my father, to my disadvantage, because he beat me up and forbade me to continue with art lessons. He said he didn't care if the clouds were white or red, but I was to stop fooling around with paint and must take up boxing lessons instead.

"I hated boxing and blocked that from my mind as well. It was at that time that I was friends with Maureen, who lived next door. She introduced me to horrible things, drink, cigarettes and *ouja* boards and weird psychic stuff. All this abuse I had buried inside me because I was in a huge muddle growing up without a mother and with a hostile, brutal father who drank and beat me and ruled me in how he thought I should live my life.

"Everything I buried deep inside my subconscious until this morning. And the flashback was so vivid and so rapid and included Maureen with her drink and cigarettes as bait. But Maureen told my father about my newly acquired vices and he nearly killed me with the thrashing he gave me."

Vivienne noticed that Ivor was visibly upset and put her arms around him.

"You are safe now, Ivor," she said. "We are together now."

Ivor was silent and breathing heavily. "And I remember she did say if she found a way to get me away from my father my repayment was to marry her when we were both eighteen. I never agreed to it. She just told me. And she did get me to a foster family from whom I ran away as they had no idea of me and my needs which weren't always physical."

He stopped talking and sat, unmoving, with Vivienne holding him. Both of them were silent, but Vivienne could feel the healing energy running from her to Ivor.

"Darling, just relax and be quiet," she said. "This has been a great shock to you, but it is in the past. Ivor. There is only this moment, you and me sitting here, safe and warm. I love you dearly and am glad for you that this revelation has occurred." Ivor just shook his head.

"Really, Ivor, it has been a missing chunk of your life. The reason you decided you would never marry. And you missed so much because of it."

Vivienne remembered that Lady Lavender had said that there was to be a flowering for him that she could help him with. This surely was what she meant.

Ivor still didn't speak. And Vivienne was quiet as well, still sitting with her arms around him. She was relieved when he gave a great sigh, then said, "You are right, Vivienne. There is only this moment and I am safe in it. I have you and, oh, how I love and appreciate you." He bent his head and kissed Vivienne. "Yes I might have missed a lot because of my messed-up childhood. but that was in the past and I only have this moment." He gave another big sigh and said tenderly, "And this moment with you, Vivienne, is so precious."

He put his arms around Vivienne and held her tight. She could feel shudders going through his body almost as if he was releasing unwanted memories. Then he gave another big sigh and gently stroked her hair.

"I am here with you in my arms," he said, as if telling himself something he didn't know. "Something I never thought I would experience. The warmth and compassion of a good woman. And you are that, Vivienne." He bent his head and kissed her again.

Vivienne was overcome with emotion. This remote, solitary man was now opening up and becoming human. Sharing his pains and sadness and coming out of it all like a surfer cresting a wave. Then almost as if he had read her thoughts he added, "Yes, I will stay on the crest of the wave and not go down into the troughs. And my darling wife, I am not ready to look at the presents you have bought for our new family in Paris, but I promise that before I go to the studio tomorrow, I will look at them. I am keen to see what we are giving them. I am so glad that I am inheriting a ready-made son, daughter-in-law and even a grandchild. What wealth, Vivienne. How can I ever thank you?"

Vivienne thought to herself, it was she who ought to be thanking him. From not wanting to stay in Kalk Bay, she now thought it the most wonderful place on earth and the best thing she could have done.

"Is all the paperwork in order for our visit to Paris?" asked Ivor.

"I will check on it tomorrow," said Vivienne. "I have finished the shopping. Now, it's just a matter of getting ourselves ready for the trip."

"And, of course," said Ivor, "I need to get ready for new students in a new studio just after we return, so I will be busy too, getting all that in order."

"Will you involve Walter and Curly at all?" asked Vivienne.

"Yes, I think so," said Ivor. "They are developing superbly. They might each like to organize a few students of their own and make use of my studio on one of the nights when I am not using it."

Vivienne was delighted. Ivor had made a rapid recovery. From being in a slump when he arrived, he had cleared out with Vivienne the traumas of his early childhood and was benefitting from the teachings she had been given that she was sharing with him. That, in doing the best to stay in the moment, dealing with current issues and not mourning a dead past.

Ivor had suffered deep trauma that day and Vivienne had endured secondary trauma by listening to him and comforting him, and both felt exhausted.

Ivor was still holding Vivienne, but his hold on her was loose now. He even smiled. "Vivienne let's have something hot to drink."

"Hot chocolate with marshmallows," suggested Vivienne.

"That sounds perfect," said Ivor. "Then let's just sit together quietly. I'm not ready to go to sleep and you are a great comfort to me."

"Perfect," Vivienne said. "Give me a few minutes to boil the kettle and top up the chocolate with marshmallows – they are decadent, aren't they?"

"Yes, they are, and do you have any crystallised melon, by any chance?"

"Oh yes, I will always have a supply of those, Ivor, as I know that is one weakness of yours."

In a very short while they sat together, not talking, just gathering strength from each other. The hot chocolate with the melted marshmallows topping it and the crystallised melon were a perfect solace.

Much later, Ivor said, "I'm ready for sleep now, Vivienne. It's been quite a day." He gave her another big bear hug.

She smiled. "I love your hugs," she said.

The next morning, Ivor had not forgotten that he wanted to see what Vivienne's shopping spree for their Paris trip had produced. He looked at the cut-glass wine glasses with a delicate rose with slender leaves around it cut into the glass and admired her choice. The red satin in which they nestled showed their beauty.

"Great choice, Vivienne," he said.

Next, she showed him the large beautiful fine linen table cloth with picture in the four corners of South African natural beauty... the harbour with yachts and fishing vessels at Kalk Bay, the majesty of Table Mountain with the sea beyond, a beach scene from Kommejie and the endearing penguins out for a swim at Boulders near Simonstown.

"I know this modern lifestyle doesn't make much use of table cloths, but there are those occasions when families gather and there is a large table laden with food and at such an occasion this cloth would be perfect."

"I agree," said Ivor, "You have picked perfect gifts. Now let's see what you have for the littlest member of the family... baby Violet."

Vivienne took the small package and opened it carefully. She had been back to fetch the engraved lapel pin and Ivor looked at it and smiled. "How clever," he said, "a perfect, very tiny, violet, but I do recognize it. In enamel on the little lapel pin. They can clip it to her bib or dress even when she is small and I should imagine she will treasure this for life. Well done, Vivienne." He bent and kissed her. Vivienne enjoyed his kisses. His beard did tickle, but that was part of loving Ivor.

In the afternoon, Ivor called Curly and Walter and suggested they run classes for students they found. Curly was delighted and Walter had good news. Cecile had stopped hounding him as his lawyer had painted a gloomy picture for her if she continued to harass him, so though there was no divorce imminent, at least, he was at peace.

"And Rose will be my first student," he said. "She's been wanting to learn how to paint."

"Great stuff," said Ivor. "And Curly you need to advertise or find students somewhere so you pass on what you have learnt from me."

"And may we ask Julie, as well?" asked Vivienne.

"Of course," said Ivor. "It has a large front room and it will be very exciting with a variety of styles from the three of us." Ivor was looking happy and Vivienne noticed a sparkle was back in his hazel eyes. The trip to Paris would be the perfect cherry on the top. This time it was Vivienne who gave Ivor a big bear hug.

"I'm only getting excited now," she said. "Now that you are living in the moment, and the exhibition was a success and you have a new gallery and we are off to a wedding in Paris. Perfectly lovely, thanks, Ivor. And all your paintings will have a home where people can view them and buy them."

Vivienne took extra care of Ivor that night. She understood how hard this must have been for him to go through. She didn't want him looking back, but she did feel he needed her support. Her strength actually. So it wasn't verbal at all. It was just being there, being aware of Ivor and his needs and tuning in to his feelings. She saw him glance at her almost like a child checking to see that his mother was close by. So, she was especially tender and caring without making Ivor aware of how she was tuning in to him. They had long periods of silence and Ivor didn't seem to want to talk much.

Then at last he said, "Thank you, Vivienne. I know you are with me heart and soul and I appreciate it. I will be much better tomorrow. Yesterday and today have been difficult. My mind keeps wanting to go back to tragedies of long ago, but I have found my peaceful head again and I will be alright.

"You can safely start preparing for the Paris trip with your lovely outfit and I'll get out my matching suit." He smiled at her. "We will be definitely visible and probably never forgotten." He caught her eye and laughed.

Vivienne was delighted. Ivor was back to being Ivor.

"Yes, before I pack them, shall we lay them out and look at them. See we have everything."

Ivor gave a mock shudder. "A deep-rose handkerchief in my pocket? I hope I don't need to use it." They both laughed and hugged one another.

Vivienne's spirits lifted. She would see the paperwork was in order, and that they had passports and visas and then, after they'd viewed their outfits, pack her suitcase for the next big step in her life. *The visit to Paris.*

# Chapter 9

They were early at the airport, and passed through the various check points and saw their luggage safely sailing down the automatic conveyor belt. A cup of coffee at a small café helped pass some time away then they were boarding the aeroplane for an overnight flight direct to Paris. Vivienne didn't much like flying, but Ivor was comfortable with it and made her feel easier. The airhostess came around with snacks and a lovely light supper soon after they were air-born. The take-off was smooth and sitting beside Ivor, Vivienne relaxed and it wasn't long before she fell asleep. She woke when it was still dark with the airhostess bringing around coffee. She rummaged in her bag for her brush to brush her hair, and after a quick bathroom break she felt almost human.

"Please return to your seats and fasten your seat belts. We are about to land in Paris," said the airhostess's voice over the loudspeaker. So Vivienne strapped herself in, and closed her eyes, feeling the plane slowly descending and waiting for the bump as the tyres of the aeroplane bounced slightly on the tarmac runway. Ivor patted her hand. "We have landed safely, my dear," he said smiling at her.

Vivienne opened her eyes. "Oh, I'm so glad," she said. "I wonder if anyone will be here to meet us, or if they will just send a taxi?"

Ivor smiled at her, and that smile said a lot.

When they were eventually through customs and with their luggage taken off the luggage carousel, they went out amongst the people waiting for the travellers, and Vivienne craned her head. *Would someone special to her be here to meet them?* She wasn't disappointed. She spied the tall slender build of her beloved son, Steven, craning his head as the travellers came to the exit.

She waved excitedly. Steven noticed and she saw the big smile on his face. She couldn't rush to him as there was a crowd of people ahead and they were pushing trolleys with their luggage, but he came to her, dodging trolleys, and they hugged. She felt as if she would never let him go. "Oh, Steven, how I've longed for this day," she said. "I'm so happy to see you." Then she turned and drew Ivor forward. She hesitated before she said it, "Steven, this is Ivor, your new step dad, and he is so happy to be part of our family."

Steven turned to Ivor and smiled widely, shaking his hand.

"What do I call you?" he asked.

Ivor smiled too but he said, "I think just call me Ivor ... what do you think?"

"Yes, and I'm Steven," said Steven.

"So, we are family. So good to meet you, Steven ... let's move on. We are holding up the traffic."

So, the three of them, pushing trolleys, went out of the airport. Vivienne's eyes were everywhere taking in the large airport, the busy people all dressed for a late-summer day.

"How are Mariette and baby Violet?" asked Vivienne.

"Both well," said Steven. "You'll be seeing them in half an hour and meeting her folks as well." He patted Vivienne's arm. "Mom, I've missed you," he said, "but I'm entirely happy, with a lovely wife to be and a darling little baby girl. You're going to love her, I know."

They had reached the large terminal where Steven's car was parked. They went up in the lift and past many cars until Steven stopped at a smart deep-blue car. He opened the boot and packed the luggage into it.

"How do you like my car, Mom," he asked. "It's the latest French car. A Citroën C6. Utter luxury. A wedding gift from my in-laws. We'll use it on the wedding."

"Steven, I'm beyond words. Congratulations. Nice car, wife to be, and family."

"Yes, it's what I've always wanted," said Steven. "And you'll meet the folks soon, too. They are hectic with wedding preparations. It's only two days away now. Quite scary, Mom," he said.

"I know," said Ivor in sympathy, "but it will be worth it, Steven. I believe you have chosen wisely."

"Oh yes, the girl of my dreams," said Steven fervently.

The traffic in Paris on this fine sunny morning was horrific and again, Vivienne closed her eyes and trusted Steven to get them safely to wherever they were going. This he did and, very shortly, Vivienne was standing outside of a stately dark wooden door, which led up a staircase to an apartment on the second floor. Very excitedly, the door flew open and a smiling Mariette was standing there, holding a small baby in her arms. The baby was dressed in baby pink with a large pale pink shawl covering most of her.

"Come inside," said Mariette to Vivienne, "and let's greet each other, then you can see baby Violet a bit better."

Inside, Mariette hugged Vivienne, who was amazed that this young girl was so loving towards her. Her heart warmed to her and she felt joy she never imagined possible, when looking at tiny Violet, who was asleep. But the tiny finger curled itself around Vivienne's finger and she felt the bond of grandmother with grandchild and smiled, close to tears.

Ivor was standing beside her and she felt his appreciation of this family event. Something new in his life she realized.

Soon, Mariette's parents came along a passage and effusively greeted both Vivienne and Ivor, who was neatly dressed and without his precious overcoat. Mariette introduced her parents as Marc and Marie. Marc had a full head of dark hair, dark eyes, and a slim moustache and Marie had fair curly hair to her shoulders and blue eyes. Both Mariette's father and mother were small in stature and smiling a gracious welcome. They were in dark clothes that declared style mattered.

"Come, Vivienne and Ivor, let us go into the lounge where I have prepared a special tea for you. But it's *café* here, unless you want tea?'

The lounge was curtained in deep-maroon velvet curtains with a view out over the roof tops of the famous city.

"Let us relax," said Marie in a delightful French accent. "You must be tired, but we have time to get to know one another."

She indicated a large sofa in a patterned material that was a relief to the dark velvet curtains, but had touches of that same colour in it. There were several armchairs in the same fabric. The table was laden with delicacies.

Baguettes camembert, brie, and ripe red tomatoes as well as crisp green basil leaves. There was also a tray of beautifully arranged petit-fours.

Marie indicated to Vivienne and Ivor to seat themselves. Her husband, Marc, sat next to her, with a genial smile on his face. Mariette and Steven sat on a small sofa for two people. Steven was holding the baby, who was asleep.

"Shall I put her in her perambulator?" asked Mariette. "Then you can better speak to your family."

"Oh, I'd love to see her before you do that," said Vivienne. "In fact I'd love to hold her."

Mariette was enchanted. "Peek at her now, Vivienne," she said, "and when she wakes, she will be so happy for her other grandmother to hold her."

She very carefully put the sleeping baby into a large pram that stood next to her.

"Now it is a great pleasure to meet Steven's mother," said Marie. "He is such a gentleman and I am so happy that my Mariette has chosen such a good man to marry."

Vivienne felt a deep sense of gratitude … for what she didn't know. For the love she had for Steven, which now he had for Mariette and she obviously had the same love for Steven.

She smiled and said to Marie, "I treasure my son and it makes me so happy that he has found his dream girl to marry."

"*Oui, Oui*, and the wedding is the day after tomorrow," said Marie. "We thought you might like to spend tomorrow sight-seeing. The famous Arch de Triumph, the Eiffel Tower, the pavement artists along the Seine River. So that you have the memories of Paris that people all over the world treasure. And you can dine at an outdoor café, so you have that experience as well."

"That sounds delightful," said Vivienne. "But don't you need some help for the wedding? We are happy to help where we can."

"*Non, non!* We have everything in hand. *merci beaucoup,*"

Marc had not spoken nor Ivor, but now Marc turned to Ivor and said, "Once, long ago, I bought a painting here and I think it was by you. It is signed Ivor M," said Marc,

"Ivor M? That's how I sign all my paintings," said Ivor in surprise. "Yes, I was a pavement artist working beside the Seine River, how exciting."

Vivienne was delighted. "How wonderful, Ivor. What a connection to you," she said, looking at Marc. "Ivor and I have only recently married."

"That is interesting," said Marc. "To marry so late! But I suppose your art has been your life companion. As I remember you were very passionate about the beautiful Seine River scene you painted. The trees reflecting in the water and people walking on the sidewalk."

"I don't remember which painting that might have been," said Ivor.

"Well," said Marc, "I can show you as I have it hanging in my office. It has such a wonderful uplifting energy and I find people, clients really, are much more amenable to talking business after they have spent a short while gazing at your painting."

Ivor laughed. "I guess Lady Lavender would go along with what you just said."

"Lady Lavender that is an interesting name," said Marie, looking intrigued.

"Oh, she's a very special lady who officiated at our small wedding."

"Speaking of weddings," said Marie, "as French people we have our own way of celebrating weddings but to honour our South African guests we have studied how you do weddings in South Africa and we will do what we can to follow the South African way. I hope you will not be disappointed that it is to be a small wedding. Just forty guests in a really special small church I have always loved, set in a garden of remembrance. And we will have a really lovely reception in a hotel that is equally special. Also quite small, but with a good reputation for quality." She looked at Vivienne. "The mother of the groom will be seated right in front in your usual tradition. On the right side on the church." She looked with affection at Mariette. "Of course, your tradition dictates that the mother of the bride will be in front on the left."

Then Steven spoke. "I wondered if Ivor might be my best man." Vivienne nearly fainted from fright. In that twin suit with the deep-rose lapels. *Wouldn't that be right out of place?* She decided to confide in Marie and the wedding party.

"I'm not so sure," she said, "I'm speaking for Ivor. We had such fun choosing clothes to wear to the wedding. Ivor has this old artist's jacket he always wears."

*"Oui,"* said Marc, "I remember it. It was a hot day and he was wearing it."

"I had a lot of trouble convincing him it was not appropriate wedding apparel," said Vivienne with a smile, "but I am not sure you will approve of what we want to wear. He might need to buy something different."

"My, that is intriguing," said Marie, "but I think your taste will be good enough."

Vivienne wasn't so sure. The trousers were nothing alarming. And the back of the jacket was likewise traditional, but the front? Maybe take out the rose handkerchief, she thought.

"We can chat about that later," said Marie. "For now, Mariette has just one small attendant. Marc's small granddaughter."

Vivienne considered that. Marc's granddaughter. Why not also Marie's granddaughter?

"She is just nine years of age," continued Marie, "with long dark ringlets and a full-length dress of pale-rose silk. She will take the bride's bouquet at the right time."

She caught Marie looking at her questioningly. "Yes, Marc has been married before," she said. "His first wife who passed away had a daughter and that granddaughter, Laurel, is his daughter's child. So, Mariette has a step-sister." She smiled at Vivienne. "Complicated families."

"All very interesting," said Ivor "and I'd love to see that painting of mine. We have so many connections."

"We can look at it straight after we've had tea," Marc said. "And I'm really pleased to have you in our family, Ivor."

Ivor was relaxing visibly, which Vivienne was pleased about. She felt comfortable with everyone and was especially looking forward to holding the still-sleeping Violet.

Marie was asking what they wanted to drink and handing out exquisite bone china small plates and indicating that they all help themselves from the plentiful arrangement on the long coffee table.

There was a lovely relaxed atmosphere that put both Vivienne and Ivor at ease.

"Now let's see the painting," said Marc. As he said this the baby began to cry.

"Shhhh," said Mariette, picking up the baby and cuddling her. Then she said to Vivienne, who was sitting on the edge of her chair, "Vivienne would you like to hold her? Just cuddle her a bit and she will stop crying."

Vivienne with her heart full of joy took the small warm bundle from Mariette and looked at the tiny face with its small quivering mouth. Ivor came to stand behind her, smiling down at the little thing.

"Shoo, don't cry, little darling," she said, moving slightly with the baby in her arms. "I'm your grandmother, sweet girl, and this here is your grandad."

The baby stopped crying and looked solemnly at her with rounded eyes. Vivienne was sure her very first granddaughter was connecting with her grandmother.

Ivor bent over and held out a finger, which the baby grasped with a little gurgle. Ivor chuckled. After a long while of billing and cooing over the babe, Vivienne gave her back to Mariette with a big smile.

"That was so special," she said.

Marc said, "Let's all go down this passage to my waiting room for clients and you will see what I mean."

It was a long corridor and it led into a large airy waiting room, painted a soft blue and with only one large painting on the end wall. The wall you immediately noticed as you entered. The painting was of the Seine River, with reflections, and with trees bending over the water, giving a feeling of protection, the trees being the protectors. The trunks of the trees caught the sunlight and there were sparkles on the leaves. The wide river was not dominating, but it was there, visible between the trees. Ivor had caught sunlight dancing off the water and sliding out from between dark areas. It had a great impact. There was peace about the tranquil scene. A peace that brought upliftment to the soul. Vivienne could see why Marc said that it put clients into an easy frame of mind and made it so easy for him to speak to them.

"Oh yes, I do remember painting this," said Ivor. "It was the last painting I did here before leaving for South Africa."

"It's wonderful, Ivor," murmured Vivienne, in approval.

"Connections, again."

"You must be tired after your air trip," said Marie. "Let me show you your room and you might like to rest. Perhaps we meet you again for lunch out at a café, say in two hours' time?"

"That would be perfect," said Vivienne.

"Yes, thank you," said Ivor.

Marie with small bustling footsteps led them to a room off that long corridor. "This is a more comfortable room than the turret room we first thought of for you to stay in. This room has an en suite bathroom," she said, "and a very comfortable bed. If there is anything you need, please let me know."

Vivienne said earnestly, "Marie, what I would really like is your opinion of Ivor's suit for tomorrow. We had fun buying it never imaging he would be Steven's best man. When I have it unpacked, can I call you to view it... and mine, too."

"*Oui,* that will be lovely," said Marie, with her charming French accent.

With that, the young couple and the parents left Ivor and Vivienne alone.

"Well, we have arrived and we have met little Violet," said Ivor.

"And you are to be best man," said Vivienne. They both laughed and hugged one another.

"We can always buy something else if they don't approve of our outfits," said Ivor.

"Well, let's lay them out on the bed then call for a viewing," said Vivienne. "Then we shall know what to do!"

Vivienne looked around the simple but stylish big bedroom. The bed covering was of quilted white, slightly shiny material. It was glamorous. Well-toned and harmonious. She breathed a sigh of relief. Steven would be in good hands, she decided.

She drew a deep breath as she opened the suitcase with their precious wedding outfits. She looked at hers first and smiled. It was flawless and couldn't be faulted. She laid it out lovingly on the bed-covering, complete with rose shoes off-white small cloth bag and headpiece with a rose on it. She stood admiring it.

"What about mine?" said Ivor. "We know you will look perfect, but what about me?"

Vivienne turned and hugged him.

"You'll look great in whatever you wear," she said. "Remember Marc knows you as the artist that painted that soothing painting in his reception area. So, I wouldn't worry, Ivor. I know they'll like it and consider it very much what an artist would wear."

She carefully lay out, next to her outfit, the one they had chosen for Ivor. The shoes were not startling. Light off white smooth leather shoes, the socks a bit of a surprise but the long off-white trousers covered them.

"So far so good," said Ivor.

"Now the shirt," said Vivienne, laying the softly salmon pink shirt onto top of the trousers.

"Perfect," she said.

"Now the tie. Softly pink with a touch of rose at the bottom. It's okay too," said Ivor. He smiled at Vivienne.

"Now for the surprise. The jacket," he said.

Vivienne carefully put the jacket on the bed with the shirt inserted and she smiled at Ivor. "The deep-rose lapels are the only startling things," she said, "and they are very slim."

"But that rose handkerchief in the pocket. Is it necessary? It is so startling."

Vivienne agreed. "Let's ask Marie and Marc what they think."

"And Steven and Mariette," added Ivor.

"Of course, them as well." So off Vivienne went in search of her host and hostess and her son and his wife to be.

Soon all were in the bedroom looking at the outfits.

"Mom, yours is elegant and outstanding," said Steven with real enthusiasm.

"And what about Ivor's? Is it suitable for a best man to wear? Let's ask Marie."

Ivor turned to Marie. "What do you think, madam?" he asked. "Is it too much of a comedy act or is it serious enough for a wedding?"

Marie smiled at Ivor and patted him on the arm. "We are so honoured to have a great artist at our daughter's wedding, and it warms my heart to see the artist is an individual and chooses to dress as he pleases. We would not ask you to change a thing, Ivor."

Ivor gave a sigh of relief and that special smile that somehow disappeared into his beard. "Vivienne and I had such an outstanding time choosing these outfits. She could have chosen more startling outfits, but this is one people will remember, don't you think?"

Marie smiled. "Yes, it has style, class."

Vivienne smiled in relief. "Now we don't need to go shopping for something different."

"Not at all," said Marie.

"So if you are ready in one hour, might we take you out to lunch, with Laurel and her parents?"

The parents and young couple left Vivienne and Ivor alone. They smiled at one another.

"Paris is turning out to be a marvellous bonding place," said Ivor. "Something I've not had in my life."

In an hour both were rested, showered and ready to go with Marc and Marie and the young couple with baby Violet in a big pram.

"We will meet Laurel and her parents at a café for late lunch," said Marie. "Then you can do a bit of sight-seeing, if you wish."

In an hour, they met with Marc's daughter, Jeanette, and her husband, Andre and their young daughter, Laurel.

Laurel was not shy. Her green eyes sparkled and her dark curls danced as she jumped excitedly when she saw Mariette. "I'm so excited, Aunt Mariette," she said.

"Laurel, this is Steven's mother, Vivienne, and his step-dad, Ivor."

"Hello," said Laurel, looking at them and smiling. "I have a long pink dress and it's so pretty," she told them.

"I have a pale-pink dress and it is pretty too," said Vivienne.

"Oh, that makes us twins," said Laurel, beaming at Vivienne.

"It does, doesn't it?" said Vivienne, smiling at the vivacious small girl.

Jeanette had held her hand out to Vivienne and Ivor. "So pleased to meet you," she said. "This is a day we have all waited for. Our special sister Mariette marrying, and such a charming young man, too. You must be sad losing him," she said to Vivienne.

By now Vivienne had very different thoughts. "Oh, not at all," she said. "He has picked the girl he has always dreamed of, so I am so happy for them, for us all, in fact."

At this warm introduction, they ordered a light meal and when they had finished, Steven and Mariette opted to go home as baby Violet had a schedule they liked to stick to. "Bath and feed and a little exercise then sleep time," said Mariette.

That left Marc and Marie and Laurel and her parents to walk with Ivor and Vivienne.

"It is pleasant to walk beside the Seine River and to look at the artists that paint there. Some sketch and paint people from life, some are pavement artists, but there is always a great atmosphere. I suggest we do that today and tomorrow you can do the other tourist stuff. Eiffel Tower is interesting if you go to the top. Quite a view of the huge area that is Paris."

So the Seine River was the afternoon's visit and proved to be the right choice. Ivor was pleased to be amongst artists and Vivienne enjoyed it, too. She reminded herself that she was becoming a real artist. Thinking like one now.

Back home, Marie's chef had cooked a wonderful roast meal and after an evening of chatting and drinking some glasses of wine, both Ivor and Vivienne slept beautifully.

Next morning after breakfast, Vivienne and Ivor went sight-seeing. They took a lift to the top of the Eiffel Tower and walked around it, taking in the breath-taking view of Paris spreading out in all directions.

Lunch at the Eiffel Tower left them free in the afternoon for a visit to the Louvre with its fabulous and famous paintings and artworks, Vivienne had seen only in pictures. To actually see them in their proper surroundings was a memorable experience.

The Arc de Triumph simply meant a taxi trip through it and a very tired Vivienne and Ivor were pleased to return to Marc and Marie's home and to enjoy another well-cooked delicious dinner.

"It's the wedding tomorrow," breathed Vivienne.

"Yes," said Marie, obviously in charge of things. "We need to be at the church at 2.30 pm so if you are ready by 2 pm that will be time enough as it is close by. Please just relax in the morning, so you are fresh for the wedding."

Vivienne decided to wash her hair and to dry it in the most stylish way she could. She and Ivor enjoyed lunch served in their room, and got dressed and ready. Vivienne smiled at Ivor. "I don't recognize this handsome man," she said, softly stroking his beard.

Ivor moved back slightly, but laughed. "I don't recognize myself. I think I could get to enjoy looking like this and dress this way every day," he said, straightening the lapel of the jacket and tucking the deep-rose handkerchief more deeply into his pocket.

"Oh, Ivor, you'd be bored in a minute," said Vivienne. "You and your artist's cloak are inseparable."

"True." Ivor smiled. "I love the way I dress and it makes it easy to paint. I would feel so restricted if I was to dress anyway else."

Vivienne breathed deeply as she slipped the heavy silk pale-salmony pink dress over her head and "Aahed," while smoothing down the sleeves. She had looked at herself in the long mirror. The way she'd blow-dried her hair had given it body and style. Her subtle makeup emphasized her blue eyes. The headdress with its rose and bit of veil looked great and then she added the jacket. She commented again on how the flared bits at the elbows in deep rose-pink matched the bodice of her dress.

"I love it, Ivor," she said.

"Darling, you look spectacular," said Ivor, "and Steven will be so proud of you."

"Ivor needs to wait in the foyer, so he can join the bridal group," said Marie. "But come, Vivienne, let me take you into the church and to the front pew."

Inside, the church had stained-glass windows and a high vaulted ceiling. It had a very reverent feel to it and, as Vivienne walked along the deep red carpet to the front pew, she felt awed. Such an important and holy time. She looked around.

The tiny church was filled with people in all kinds of beautiful outfits. Their own outfits were special, but not outlandish. She was deeply glad they had bought what they did.

She sat in the front pew and waited until the wedding music played and she turned briefly to see Mariette in an elegant, but simple dress of heavy white satin with a heart-shaped neckline and three-quarter sleeves. Marc was walking his daughter down the aisle, and had her gloved hand on his arm. Laurel was walking behind her in a long dress almost the colour of Vivienne's and her dark curls bounced slightly as she walked. And then they had reached the mayor of the town who was to perform the ceremony.

It began and was conducted in French. Vivienne was proud of the way Steven said his vows in flawless French. Vivienne was tearful as the young couple made their vows. One quick glance showed Marie was dabbing at her eyes.

The mayor said in accented English to Steven, "You may now kiss ze bride."

Vivienne was so filled with emotion as she saw the tender way her son bent forward to kiss Mariette. She could sense the intense love he had for this vivacious young French woman. She saw the way that Mariette looked at Steven and knew for certain this was a union of two hearts meant for each other. She knew a sense of joy that she genuinely was happy her son was now married and had left her hearth and home and would make one of his own, here in France. She felt tears welling up in her eyes, but they were unshed tears. And after the groom kissed the bride, the mayor ushered them into the vestry to sign the marriage register, she could sense the emotion of all present.

Vivienne glanced around briefly.

The small church was crowded with people in immaculate attire, all very elegant, and she knew without doubt that she could easily fit into the classy atmosphere, and so would Ivor, accepted with reverence as an artist from South Africa.

Soon, the bride with her veil off her face and a look of great happiness on it, with an adoring groom and a bridal party of small Laurel carrying a basket of rose petals and Ivor, the best man, made its way out of the vestry and down the red carpet in the church. The congregation followed in a tight group behind them and when they reached the door leading outside, a photographer asked the bridal group to stand for a moment, whilst he took some pictures. Then young Laurel with her basket of rose petals, her long dark curls bouncing and wearing a huge smile threw rose petals into the well-wishers.

The sun was shining. The sky a lovely shade of blue and there was just enough of a slight breeze to make the day comfortable. Vivienne watched as the bridal group got into a stylish car with a "just married" banner floating in the air above it. She smiled. Yes, just married and off to the reception now, she walked with Marie to a waiting car and was whisked off briskly to a small but classy hotel a block away.

Inside the décor was in pale pink with roses. "Same as my dress," breathed Laurel, who had caught up with Vivienne and Marie. Ivor was smiling as he towered over his small wife.

"I've never enjoyed myself so much," he said to her softly. His twinkling hazel eyes were full of joy. "I never thought I could fit into such a scene, but it filled some empty spaces in me. Truly delightful."

Vivienne was glad as ushers showed them into the reception room. There was a large table for the bridal couple and bride and groom's parents and the little flower girl, and a beautiful high tiered wedding cake in the middle of the table. Soon the small gathering was seated and speeches began. Ivor looked nonplussed.

"Haven't got a speech," he whispered to Vivienne.

*Just talk,* she mouthed back.

And there was warmth and sincerity amongst the small gathering. Short speeches from the heart, with Ivor's being genuine with the small bit of humour he most often brought to any conversation.

Champagne corks popped, people were toasting the young couple, and music played as Steven and Mariette took to the small circular dance floor. Vivienne sighed. They were a perfect couple, Steven, tall slender and blond and Mariette, short, dark-haired with that flawless complexion and big blue eyes. She was so glad they had made the trip here.

Soon other dancers were on the floor, Ivor was dancing with small Laurel, his big feet awkwardly making sure they didn't stand on her tiny silver shoes. Soon Laurel smiled at him and dropped out, and Ivor indicated to Vivienne that she join him. Not a lot of people were on the dance floor at that time and it was a slow waltz that Ivor could manage. Vivienne let him lead her and felt warm and secure and she chuckled inwardly to herself. In their matching outfits on a dance floor in Paris. What would her three friends say now? That was a fleeting thought, but one she knew she must complete when home by ringing each of them to tell them how much better it was here, that it wasn't just the coffee and that nothing happens by chance.

It was such a beautiful wedding and happy reception that both Ivor and Vivienne enjoyed. Vivienne had never seen Ivor this relaxed and happy.

She remembered that Lady Lavender had told her she was to help Ivor to flower as there were huge blank spaces in his life that might have been filled with laughter and joy, but he had never had that chance.

Now he danced with Vivienne and enjoyed chatting to Marc and Marie. Vivienne didn't need him to tell her he was enjoying this new aspect of his life. She could see he was and she felt glad that maybe this lovely outfit she was wearing might get some activity when they got home.

Home. She realised that the time with Steven, Mariette and her family was almost over and they would be leaving for home on the day after next.

"Vivienne, there is so much at stake," Ivor had said. "The new gallery needs to be fitted out and the new students will lose interest if I don't start lessons as soon as we get home."

Vivienne knew that side of Ivor. The committed artist and this was the side that Lady Lavender also wanted to see Ivor develop. There was a definite power in his paintings and if he passed that knowledge onto students, of the method of painting without thought, of knowing one's pallete so well that the brush inherently went into the perfect colour for whatever was to appear next on his watercolour paper; he would help humanity with this precious knowledge.

So, the next day went quickly and very soon they were saying emotional farewells to Steven, Mariette and baby Violet, who Vivienne was sure had bonded with her. Marc and Marie were also sincere in their good wishes as Steven whisked them off the airport to begin the trip home.

On the plane, Vivienne had a window seat. She sat looking at the banks of white clouds, looking so solid as if one could walk on them or, better still, lie on them. She was in a dreamy state of mind and then unexpectedly she thought of Lady Lavender. And all the help both she and Ivor had had from her. Without her input, this wonderful journey and this darling man sitting next to her would not have happened. She had been too much wound up in herself, too judgmental, and definitely too tied to Steven. She had learnt to let all that go and, better still, she had learnt to live in the moment, such a moment as now, when she was looking out of a plane window at the vastness of the universe and she turned to Ivor and said, "The first thing we are doing when we get home, Ivor, is to visit Lady Lavender."

# Chapter 10

Back in Kalk Bay, Vivienne said, "It all looks so familiar, I don't feel I've left here at all."

"You just have to look at the pictures you took to remember we have been on a magical journey and had magical things happen," said Ivor, smiling at Vivienne.

"I know my outfit wants to get out some more," said Vivienne.

"Oh yes, and the next time you wear it will be in a very few days' time," said Ivor. "I am going to work really hard at setting up the studio with my paintings from my lounge at home, and with the new ones we did at the exhibition. I painted ten, all very nice, just need framing."

"And I painted six," said Vivienne. "Also need framing."

"Will you see to that tomorrow?" said Ivor. "We will have a grand opening in a week's time. You in your outfit."

Vivienne smiled, "And you in yours, Ivor. It will be perfect."

"But before I get to the framers, you and I are visiting Lady Lavender in the morning, and telling her all these lovely things," said Vivienne.

"Which she already knows," said Ivor.

"She is too much of a lady to spoil my fun," said Vivienne. "I just feel she needs to know how much we appreciate all her advice, some of which I didn't appreciate at the time."

So the next morning, Ivor and Vivienne went down the little twisty lane and around the corner to see the charming fisherman's cottage with its slightly crooked walls and chimney and the big brass knocker on the door.

"Right, my darling wife, you knock."

So Vivienne did and quite quickly the door was opened. There stood Lady Lavender in a long yellow dress that seemed to give off light.

She looked at Vivienne and Ivor with a very gentle expression. Her deep-set gimlet eyes were soft as she said, "Come in, my dears, I have been expecting you. And you know the drill – kitchen first then with ginger tea and apple cookies we go to the lounge for a good old chat."

Vivienne and Ivor followed her into the kitchen. Vivienne looked up at the now-familiar wooden beams that held up the thatched roof, and watched as Lady Lavender brewed the ginger tea and opened a tin of apple cookies. The smell of cake and apple wafted up and Vivienne smiled.

Lady Lavender saw and said, "Yes, Vivienne, they taste as nice as they smell. Now let us head to the lounge:"

In the lounge, lazily lying on a chair was the big black cat. "Captain, do you mind sharing the couch with me," said Lady Lavender to the cat. "We have visitors who would like to sit on the chairs."

The big black cat obligingly stretched, stood up and made a leap from the chair onto the end of the couch.

"Please be seated," said Lady Lavender with a rare smile. "This is a great pleasure as I see you are both in a great new place."

Vivienne looked at Ivor, puzzled.

"Now - not physically," said Lady Lavender, "but you have both sprouted wings and flown to great heights. This is the work that I do and to see it playing out so wonderfully fills me with delight.

"However, please drink your tea and sample the apple cookies and then you need to fill me in as to why I see you in such a wonderful space."

Ivor and Vivienne did as instructed and as soon as Vivienne was ready, she said, "Lady Lavender, Ivor and I both wanted to come and thank you for all the wonderful things that have been happening for us." She took a breath. "And they wouldn't have happened without your help."

"Yes," said Ivor, "last time we were here you gave me a few packets with leaves and bits of twig to make into a drink to swallow."

Lady Lavender smiled. "You are so graphic, Ivor. I know what you are saying and did it help?"

"Oh yes, the salt in the corners of the rooms cleared the atmosphere so that it was light and pleasant and that drink of leaves and stems was not pleasant."

"It was not meant to be pleasant," said Lady Lavender, "but didn't it do the trick?"

"Oh yes," said Ivor. "I vomited heartily. It was exhausting."

"That's good," said Lady Lavender. "That would have got rid of most of the evil psychic links that that woman had put into you."

"Really, it sounds horrible," said Ivor.

"That woman meant business, Ivor," said Lady Lavender. "You are lucky to have escaped … and did you do the inhaling in the morning?"

"Yes I did," said Ivor, "and after I got such a feeling of peace and joy."

"That's what I like to hear," said Lady lavender. "That is my spiritual work – to help clear evil away and allow light to enter dark spaces."

"I've felt much lighter and happier ever since," said Ivor.

"And Vivienne had a job to do, which I am sure Ivor doesn't mind knowing."

"And that was?" asked Ivor.

"That was to support you, Ivor," said Lady Lavender. "To be there as your rock, your stability. I know you are a well-balanced and centred person but there is so much that you have missed out on that most humans enjoy during their lifetimes. That bucket needed to be filled. But maybe you have a report on that, Vivienne?"

Vivienne knew very well that Lady Lavender knew everything, but she duly reported, "Perhaps we should start with the day of the painting exhibition," she said. "Ivor has got a list of students who want classes and then I met with a man who offered Ivor a venue. A gallery of his own."

"Good news," said Lady Lavender. "And where is this gallery?"

"Believe it or not," said Ivor, "it's in Main Street, just a few doors away from where we live."

"Marvellous," said Lady Lavender.

"So, my framed paintings of which I have many, will go in there and..."

Vivienne broke in. "...Ivor will be teaching students there and two of his students will be doing the same as well."

"And we are getting publicity on radio and newspaper," said Ivor.

"Even better," said Lady Lavender. "Your bucket is filling very well, Ivor. I can see the people whose lives you are touching ,,, new students, too. That is good news. And I did ask Vivienne to help and support you."

"Oh, she has been doing that," said Ivor. "She even took me shopping for a suit to wear to the Paris wedding."

"Yes, and you two have been to Paris," said Lady Lavender.

"The outfits we chose are matching sets. A bit outlandish, but Ivor is an artist and he couldn't wear what he normally wears."

Ivor smiled and drew his loose coat more closely around him.

"I agree there," said Lady Lavender, smiling at Ivor. "You are appropriately dressed for an artist at home, but for a Paris wedding, you would have needed to look part of the wedding scene."

"We did very well, Lady Lavender."

"How wonderful," said Lady Lavender.

Ivor was smiling. "Yes, I had big chunks of my life missing though I had a sudden insight to a lot of my earlier life which took adjusting to … Vivienne helped me get through that bad patch. Yes, I had lost a lot when it comes to social events and people. And that day of the wedding I was part of a happy occasion I had never thought I'd experience."

"And," said Vivienne, "I know what you have done to help me get my thoughts under control, to remember to stay in the present moment, and yes, I have succeeded rather well."

"I can see you have been there for Ivor, just as I asked you to, Vivienne, so from my side I am delighted with your progress and that of Ivor."

"We have an opening for our gallery in a few days' time. Would you like to come, Lady Lavender?" asked Vivienne.

Lady Lavender smiled. "My dear, thank you for the invitation. I will be there in spirit though you won't see me. I'm sure you understand that I do not go to physical events, but stay here in this cottage where I am in touch with events in the universe. I am able to help clear away the negative energies of tragedies and unhappy events. and even to help people with heavy hearts to feel lighter, happier.

"It has been my great pleasure to have helped you, Vivienne, to help yourself, and to help Ivor, a strong man, who nevertheless needs the compassion of a good woman, someone to share joys with, a good friend, there in all circumstances. And you, Ivor, with those splendid new wings you have – your painting will bring smiles and joy to people, who hang your paintings in their homes or work places. And the students you are developing will do the same and the world will be a better place because you are in it.

"That is my little piece for today, so you see, Vivienne, no lectures."

Vivienne knew one didn't hug people like Lady Lavender, but that's what she felt like doing. *What a very special person she was.* So, she looked Lady Lavender in the eye and she knew in that look Lady Lavender would read her very grateful thanks for the joy that was now in her life.

The big black cat had done his usual 'your visiting time is over act'. He stood up, stretched and jumped off the sofa.

Vivienne smiled. "Thanks for the reminder, Captain. And thank you, Lady Lavender for your time."

Ivor stood up and gave Lady Lavender a slight bow. Then he looked at her and smiled. "I am so glad Vivienne brought me to see you. I had heard …"

"Yes, that I am a witch," said Lady Lavender with a smile.

"Well, yes," said Ivor, "but I know what a wonderful gifted woman you are and I thank you from the bottom of my heart."

"You will visit again," said Lady Lavender. "But it will be more like today. No more lessons and lectures."

"We will enjoy that," said Vivienne. Captain had brushed meaningfully against them. "Oh, yes, thanks again and we will follow you, Captain."

She saw Lady Lavender watching them with a tender expression on her face.

"We are going to have such fun with our lives," said Vivienne.

"Yes, I can see that," said Ivor. "The gallery will add another dimension to what we do."

"Ah, an afternoon function will be better for you," said Vivienne. "That suit is not one to wear at night, but will be great for an opening of an art gallery."

"Shall we say at three pm? Saturday coming? We will let the local newspaper and radio know to invite visitors."

"We can lay on a nice tea," said Vivienne..

"Oh yes," said Ivor, "with champagne in champagne glasses and non-alcoholic champagne for those who don't drink."

It was all very exciting and, for the next few days, Ivor did no painting, but a lot of carting of paintings from his home studio to the developing gallery in Main Street.

Julie also drove over with a selection of six of her best studio photographs in large frames, all matching, and all with her flair for drama of backlighting putting black-and-white photography into an elegant gallery with serious paintings.

Vivienne took out her pale salmony pink dress with matching jacket.

"I think I'll invite the assistant who helped us to choose these outfits," she said.

"We can also have a few people painting in the room at the back," said Ivor. "Maybe Curly can arrange that. Or Walter."

There was a great deal of activity in this new gallery with window dressing of a few of Ivor's best paintings. Ivor brought in chairs for people to sit on and a couple of small tables. He arranged for a very large table to be delivered for drinks and nice eats for visitors to his opening.

The chaos in that empty shop as Ivor's small team worked at getting things ready soon turned it into a gallery with a great feel to it. One of warmth and upliftment.

"Just what Marc said about the painting of yours that he bought," said Vivienne. "This new gallery has a great feel to it. And I like the signage outside that simply says: *Ivor Art of Main Street.* You will need to make a speech."

"If you make one, too," said Ivor. "We'll jointly make the opening speech at three pm with drinks and snacks straight away. Then people can look at the paintings and book for classes."

All went to plan, and wearing their matching outfits, Vivienne smiled at Ivor a half an hour before the opening. In his arty suit with slim rose lapels and his slightly shorter hair he looked inspiring.

"This is going to be such a special day, Ivor," she said.

"We are a great team ..." Ivor bent and kissed his wife.

Everything went to plan. Visitors enjoyed the champagne and non-alcoholic drinks and plentiful eats. The new art gallery was a welcome addition to the shops already there.

Vivienne and Ivor stayed until the last visitor had left. The sun was sinking and a pink and golden glow lit up the view of the sea beyond the houses.

Vivienne smiled.

*"This is our triumph...Simple but stunning,"* she said to Ivor, adding, *"Nothing happens by chance. Isn't that what Lady Lavender said?"*

Printed in the United States
by Baker & Taylor Publisher Services